Anton and Cecil

Anton and Cecil
Cats at Sea

By LISA MARTIN *and*
VALERIE MARTIN

Illustrated by KELLY MURPHY

ALGONQUIN YOUNG READERS 2013

Published by
Algonquin Young Readers
an imprint of Algonquin Books of Chapel Hill
P.O. Box 2225
Chapel Hill, NC 27514-2225

a division of
Workman Publishing
225 Varick Street
New York, New York 10014

LIBRARY OF CONGRESS CATALOGING-IN-PUBLICATION DATA
Martin, Lisa, [date]
Anton and Cecil : cats at sea / by Lisa Martin and Valerie Martin ; illustrated
by Kelly Murphy.—First edition.
pages cm
Summary: The high-seas adventures of two cat brothers.
ISBN 978-1-61620-246-0
[1. Cats—Fiction. 2. Brothers—Fiction. 3. Seafaring life—Fiction.
4. Adventure and adventurers—Fiction.] I. Martin, Valerie, [date]
II. Murphy, Kelly, [date] illustrator. III. Title.
PZ7.M36354An 2013
[Fic]—dc23   2013008475

10 9 8 7 6 5 4 3 2 1
First Edition

For our dearest shipmates,
Cole, Cabot, and Calliope.
Anchors aweigh!

CONTENTS

Anton *and* Cecil

CHAPTER 1

The Harbor at Lunenburg

The herring slapped onto the wooden dock as the men shook the nets to free the last of them. Anton and Cecil watched from the shadows between stacks of crates. This was the crucial moment, before the men began scooping the fish into containers and hauling them away. One of the catch, larger than most, flopping helplessly, slithered from the top and careened down the side of the quivering pile of fish. Cecil shifted his weight to his back paws, his muscles tensed.

Anton moved slightly to block him. "Not yet," he breathed, but Cecil sprang from the crates and in two long bounds reached the fish. He clamped its tail between his jaws and turned sharply, dragging the squirming weight, skidding on the slippery wood. A fisherman grunted and lunged for the fish. He caught its slick gills for a moment before it slid through his fingers. Cecil pulled hard, breaking into a run as the man turned to give chase.

Now Anton darted from the hiding place, eyes wide and intent upon a smaller herring at the bottom of the pile. A fat rubber boot stomped the dock behind him, narrowly missing his tail. He leaped across the pile, scrambling wildly over the churning fish, finally bolting through the closing circle of boots, empty-jawed.

Crouched behind the nearest tower of coiled ropes, Anton listened for pursuers but heard only rough laughter as the men returned to the catch. He trotted along a dirt path lined with scrub weeds, arriving at an old lighthouse perched on the edge of a jumble of flat rocks overlooking the ocean. Slipping between two loose boards on the lighthouse's foundation, he let his eyes adjust to the dim light inside, carefully stepped around the weathered wooden posts, and stopped, looking at Cecil.

Cecil glanced up, motionless, then returned

to cleaning his back paw. The herring lay stiff on the dry stone at his side. "So," he said, his voice slightly mocking, "where's yours?"

Anton crouched on the rock slab and folded his tail neatly alongside him. "Hmph," he snorted. "After the scene you made, there wasn't much chance for me to get one, was there? So much for *sneaking.* Next time, I go first!" He lowered his eyelids as if he were bored.

Cecil finished cleaning his paw and turned to his catch, chuckling. "If you'd gone first we'd still be waiting for you to choose one." With his sharp teeth and claws, he ripped a chunk of flesh from the fish and tossed it to his brother. Anton sniffed the fish carefully, then began to chew small mouthfuls. "It's like I always tell you, little kit," said Cecil, his cheeks bursting with herring. "Don't be a chicken, be a cat! Be adventurous!"

Anton scooped up the last morsel and rose to leave. "Thanks for lunch," he called as he slipped back out between the boards. *But not for the advice,* he thought, narrowing his eyes. Cecil was good at many things—hunting and stealing and muscling his way through. But every cat couldn't be like Cecil. And every cat didn't need to hear about it.

As Anton rounded the bend in the lighthouse path, he looked out upon the busy port of his home village. The harbor, full of stately tall ships resting at anchor, resembled a forest of leafless trees. Ships with masts as tall as houses, their spars stretching like arms out past the massive hulls, bobbed at anchor as far as the eye could see. The big brigs and three-masted barques in which humans sailed the world plowed toward the docks from the open sea, slow and ponderous as elephants, while the smaller fishing schooners, quick as rabbits, darted into the harbor at dawn, returning in the evening loaded down with hills of shivering silver fish, lobsters as big as platters, nets heaped with oysters, mussels, and clams. The brightly painted shops and houses of the town, built in tiers on a steep slope, looked down upon the waterfront like an audience eager to see a show. And what a show it was, from dawn to dusk.

When the tall ships sailed into the harbor, past the breakwater and up to the docks, many interesting things were disgorged. First came the sailors, intriguing in their own right, with their colorful scarves and sashes and boisterous manners. Then they unloaded the ship's deep hold. Out came great sacks of flour, metal pipes, wooden carriage wheels, crates of miniature trees with odd-shaped leaves, cows, goats, and sheep, roped together, balking at the gangway, mooing and bleating. There were wooden barrels of all sizes, pallets laden with bales of cotton and wool, skids of bricks and lumber, cages of chickens, huge blocks of ice.

All of it was in constant motion, pushed and pulled by the bustling stevedores who plied their barrows and carts through the ranks of horse-drawn carriages on the docks, past the shouting sailors and the occasional bevy of weeping ladies there to welcome their husbands and their sons. A ceaseless chorus of noise accompanied the mayhem: shouting men, rollicking children, the joyful barking of aimless dogs, the cries of the seagulls rising in squads to circle the town or dive into the harbor, the screech of osprey, the yowling of the town's resident cats.

Some of the sailors scoffed at the cats, while others gave them a kind word, or even tossed a fish too small or too bony for their own uses. The sailors were not surprised to see the cats, nor were the cats perturbed by the sailors, though they were wary of them, for good reason. But where there are sailors and ships and the sea, there are fish and mice and rats, and where there are fish and mice and rats, there are cats. It has always been so. Humans long to cross the sea, to visit strange lands and see wonders undreamed of. Cats—well, most cats—do not.

Anton and Cecil were brothers born in a cozy recess beneath the old lighthouse perched on the rocky breakwater that curves out from the harbor. Their mother, Sonya, was young when her sons were born; they were her first litter. Like her, Anton was svelte, elegant, and gray as a storm cloud. He was cautious and sensitive by nature, and picky about food. He liked to plan ahead.

Cecil was black with white forepaws, a paint-brush of white at the end of his tail, and startling white whiskers (their father was a stylish tuxedo cat from the town). He was big, beefy, goofy, and omnivorous. Cecil was curious about everything, but especially about ships and the sea. The sailors never saw enough of Anton to give him a name, but Cecil, who liked to sit on the dock in the sun, gazing at the sea like a pensive jack of spades, they called "Blackjack."

As kittens the brothers were of a size, but Cecil

had big paws and his fur was longer and silkier than Anton's gray coat, which took no time at all for Sonya to clean. Cecil grew taller and heavier, outstripping his brother and then his mother, and then every other cat on the wharf. He was always hungry, and there was nothing he wouldn't eat. Often a river of mice streamed from the ships looking for new haunts after their journey. Cecil devoured any he could manage to pounce on, even if they made his belly ache for hours afterward. Anton was nimble enough to trap mice in his paws, to let them go and trap them again, but he did it for sport. He simply had no taste for mice. Another treat Cecil enjoyed, to his fastidious brother's horror, was water beetles.

"They're good," Cecil claimed. "They're crunchy."

"Ugh," said Anton. "I'd rather wait for a fish."

Sonya was a loving mother, and having only two sons meant she had more time to teach them everything she knew about life in the lighthouse, in the town, and on the wharf. The brothers were both fascinated by the bustle of sailors on the waterfront, but Sonya warned them of the dangers of being impressed into service on a ship. "They come on the dock at night, and if they see a cat, they tempt him with fish and then scoop him up and throw him in the hold until the ship is out to sea. Some are never seen again. I knew an old fellow who came back and said he'd seen the world."

"And what did he see?" asked Cecil.

"Horrible sights. Humans had fur and swung in trees."

"Frightening," Anton agreed.

"Interesting," said Cecil, wide-eyed. "I'd like to see that."

"And he'd seen a country made of nothing but sand."

"Flat or hilly?" asked Cecil.

"Who cares?" said Anton. "Right here is the best place in the world for a cat to live. Everybody says that."

"That's true," agreed Sonya. "Everyone says that. Even those who have gone away and come back again."

During the day, Anton, the more thoughtful brother, preferred to spend his nap times close to Sonya in the lighthouse, snuggled on the old quilt where he'd been born. In the evenings, though, the music from the saloon in town drew him out of hiding to slip quietly through the chill alleys, following the trail of marvelous sounds. He'd found a broken board in the wall of the saloon storeroom, with just enough space to squeeze through. The door into the bar was usually left ajar, and he discovered that he could sit behind it and hear the instruments and the singing well enough. Closing his eyes and curling his paws, he often purred loudly with pleasure as the music rumbled in his rib cage.

One evening, Anton said to Cecil, "You could come with me tonight to hear some music," but Cecil smiled and shook his head.

"Nope, I've got more exciting things to do," he said as he stalked off, disappearing into the dark. Anton shivered looking after him, hardly daring to think of the mischief he might be up to.

While Anton was out salooning, Cecil climbed the dusty wooden stairs to the top of the lighthouse and sat by the railing, gazing out at the ocean. The bitterly cold wind blew his fur and stung his eyes, but he was content to stay there for hours, smelling the scents of the sea, watching the waves. Sometimes he could see the sails of tall ships moving slowly, mysteriously along the horizon. Tonight, the moon was bright, and he glimpsed a pod of whales playing far from shore. He watched until they faded silently from his view.

❖ ❖ ❖

A white cat, pale and ghostly in the moonlight, sat on a low wharf near the shore looking down at the silvery shapes in the water. Black fur masked her eyes and ears, a petite thief in the dark night. The high tide pooled within a ring of rocks, presenting a deep bowl of darting fish, quite catchable in her estimation, though admittedly she was young and optimistic in these matters. She crouched low and stretched one pearly paw slowly over the water, extending her claws, cocking her head in an effort to track the path of the swirling fish. A steady breeze off the harbor rustled the leaves in the scrub bushes, waves lapped up on the rocky shoreline, and wooden dock planks creaked and sighed behind her.

She focused on the fish, so near, and tensed for the strike. A wisp of a scent passed under her nose—it seemed out of place. Was it . . . rubber? She twisted sharply around in time to glimpse a short, grubby sailor throw something through the air toward her. She sprang away from him with a shriek, but too late; the fish net landed heavily over her. Rising up on hind legs she struggled, tearing at the netting with her teeth and claws as the sailor rushed to her. A small hole opened in the mesh, big enough to jam a paw through, but the sailor swiftly gathered the edges and scooped her up, grinning through yellowed teeth as he held the net bag high enough to peer at her.

The trapped cat howled frantically as she swung in the netting alongside the sailor's heavy boots. Whistling a tune as though pleased with himself, the sailor walked down the length of the dock and up a gangway toward a waiting ship. The cat scrambled desperately to right herself in the net, pivoting around her paw, which was still awkwardly thrust through the netting. She shifted her weight to her hindquarters, pushed her free foreleg out as far as it would go, and slashed at the sailor's leg. The sailor yelped and cursed as her claws ripped through his dungarees into the skin below. Instead of dropping the net as she had hoped, however, he thumped it savagely against a railing, leaving her dazed and mewling in pain and anger.

Up on deck the sailor approached a wide hatch-way. The cat heard the click and whine of a door unlatched and opened. The fish net was loosened, her ghost-white body dumped onto a dusty floor. The door slammed shut, then blackness. Silence.

CHAPTER 2

A Cat at Sea

Aye! It's Blackjack, there's our boy!" The fishermen called to Cecil as he made his way along the docks to his favorite sunning spot, though the sun had only just risen over the horizon. Cecil settled himself next to a pier post to block the wind off the harbor and looked around at the scene.

The three-masted schooners rode high in the water while the men wound up the nets and ropes and prepared to set the sails. Cecil had seen many of the sailors before and knew them by their clothes and the sounds of their gruff voices. The short one with wide shoulders always wore a headscarf the color of the sky on a clear day, while another was tall with a threadbare red wool cap that had seen many voyages. The headscarf man called out instructions to the hustling deckhands, and from time to time he glanced over at Cecil.

"Our Blackjack there, he seems a lazy one, don't he?" he said to his companion, who grunted.

"A nice life, looks like to me," the red cap man answered, stopping for a moment to gaze at the black cat.

Cecil saw them looking at him, though he understood nothing they said, and a tickle of excitement ran through him. *Were they talking about him?* He stood and stretched his back into a high arch. *What were they saying?* He looked into their faces and over at the schooner. The big ships went out to sea and sometimes never came back, but Cecil knew that the fishing schooners returned every day; the crewmen wouldn't impress cats on those. *They might be saying, "That cat would make an excellent sailor, he would."* The thought was thrilling. He took a few steps toward the men and uttered a short, questioning mew at them.

"Oh, ho, Ben Fox!" said the red cap man. "Looks as if the cat is wantin' somethin' from us."

Cecil approached the ship haltingly, tail and head low, until he reached the long wooden plank, which stretched from the dock to the deck of the schooner. Tentatively he put his paw on the edge and looked back at the two men. Sailors carrying fishing gear and trawl lines swerved to avoid tromping on him, and the ship's bobbing made the plank sway unnervingly. From over the side of the ship there suddenly appeared another man's face, with light green eyes that reminded Cecil of Anton's, and a thin triangle of fur on his chin.

"Well, mates!" he bellowed down to the other two men, who jumped and ran forward. "Quit your yappin'! We're burnin' daylight!" He caught sight of Cecil and his green eyes narrowed. "Keepin' pets now are we, Mr. Fox?"

This yelling man didn't seem to be a fan of his, and Cecil crouched, immobile, ready to bolt but still desperate to get on the ship. One of the passing seamen swung his boot to kick Cecil off the plank, but Ben blocked him.

"Cap'n, sir!" Ben called up. "Permission to bring aboard this excellent mouser." The captain's eyebrows shot up and he opened his mouth to retort, but Ben quickly added, "and black as he is, he's bound to bring us good luck." This was a clever point to make, since sailors always liked to have a black cat aboard to ensure a safe voyage—"unlucky on land, lucky at sea" was the saying—and ship captains were especially concerned with omens and luck. The bustling fishermen paused and all eyes appraised Cecil, who was still poised with his paw on the plank.

The captain pressed his lips together for a silent moment, then barked out, "Mr. Fox, give the creature a trial if you must, but if he steals as much as an eyeball of my catch, you'll be answerin' for him, you will!" And he withdrew his head from the deck rail.

Ben beamed at Cecil and stood to one side of the plank, gesturing upward. "Got yer chance, Blackjack. Let's get to boardin' now. Step lively." Shaking with excitement, Cecil gave Ben a long look and slunk up the plank with quick paws, turning sharply into the nearest shadow when he reached the deck. The deck smelled deliciously fishy; the wooden timbers creaked under the weight of the busy crew. *I'm here!* thought Cecil, astonished. *I'm sailing!*

Rough hands pushed the heavy plank out to the dock and others untied the thick mooring ropes.

Cecil felt the ship shudder and then move freely. From behind the barrels he rose up on his hind legs, reaching with his front paws until he could just peek over the side through a gap under the blackened railing. There was the dock, sliding away, then the breakwater gliding past, as Cecil's golden eyes flicked left and right at the sights. High above him the sailors dropped the thick white sails and they began to catch the breeze. Cecil scrambled onto a low barrel for a better view. Exhilarated and strangely calm, he felt the wind pull on his fur, and he could see it filling the sails stretched across the masts. The push of the schooner against the waves made a rhythm deep in his belly.

As they rounded the tip of the land and the ocean spread out in front of them, Ben stomped up with folded lengths of netting draped across his shoulders.

"Now Blackie my lad, eat the rats, not the catch, got that?" He shook his thick finger at Cecil, who watched him seriously. Ben gave him a heavy pat on the back and stomped off again. Cecil decided this meant that things were settled for now and returned to gazing at the widening sea before him.

❖ ❖ ❖

Anton sat on the brick apron of the lighthouse with his tail curled around and over his back feet and began to clean his face. He squeezed his eyes shut as he dragged his wet paw across them and then licked the paw again, enjoying the morning ritual as the sunshine warmed the bricks. Moving on to his ears, Anton glanced up at the passing gulls and over at a fishing schooner in the harbor. With one ear pinned flat against his forehead under his cleaning paw, he stopped and stared. There was a cat sitting on a barrel on the deck of the boat. Anton dropped his paw. The cat was huge and jet black . . . Anton stretched his neck forward. The cat on the boat turned his head to look at one of the fishermen. It was *Cecil*! Sailing away! Anton rushed to the edge of the rock wall. Oh *no*! Cecil had been captured and forced out to sea! Anton dashed back and forth along the wall, crying out in frustration. The ship was moving rapidly, leaving no way for him to call out or signal to Cecil. He mewed brokenly and stood still, watching the tall sails of the schooner billowing in the distance.

❖ ❖ ❖

Late in the afternoon, when Cecil, reeking of fish, strode smugly down the plank and onto the dock, Anton was furious.

"Where have you been?" he howled at Cecil, who trotted past the mooring posts, examining the size of other ships' catches for the day. "What were you thinking? You could have been drowned or stolen!" Anton insisted, running in little bursts to keep up with Cecil. "I've been worried to death!"

Cecil turned for a last glance at "his" schooner, flicked his tail, and sat down to face Anton, who plowed directly into him. "I wasn't stolen. I was invited aboard," explained Cecil, placing his paw squarely against his brother's nose to back him up a bit. "Don't you even want to know how it was?" he asked.

"No," huffed Anton, circling around Cecil to check that he was intact, licking his slimed fur in a few places. He finally sat down and gave in. "Okay," he said with a sigh. "How was it?"

"Glad you asked!" said Cecil happily, and he began by explaining how the captain had rolled out the welcome mat for him.

✤ ✤ ✤

Old Billy, the harbormaster's cat, relished his reputation at the docks as the one who knew all about ships, sailors, and the wide world. True, he had never gone to sea; he'd gone soft in the belly and was no longer a mouser of any distinction. But in his years of service to the harbormaster he had heard many tales of foreign lands and cats, some delightful, some dark and dreadful. One of his duties, he felt, was to pass on news of import to his fellow felines, and it was for this reason that he sat resolutely on the dock that evening and relayed again and again the story of what he had seen to any who stopped by. Anton was standing toward the back of the crowd.

Billy had been awakened the night before from his bed in the master's small house by a yowling outside, and had scrambled to the windowsill in time to see a dismaying scene. A sailor unknown to Billy was climbing a gangplank carrying a sack of gathered netting, and in the sack appeared to be (and here he paused meaningfully) a small cat. The assembled crowd groaned; this was not at all unheard of, but always distressing. Billy described in vivid terms how the cat bravely thrust its paw through the mesh to slash at the sailor, and how it was cruelly repaid.

Anton shuddered. Even though his brother had gone willingly, even happily, on one of the daily fishing jaunts, Anton still felt a deep worry in his bones about these other disappearances. Sonya had called it being *impressed* into service, stolen right off the docks. Anton felt a little ill thinking of how it might happen to any cat, at any time.

"Well for goodness' sake, Bill, who was it, could you tell?" asked an older female anxiously.

"I couldn't see a face, I'm afraid." Billy shook his head gravely.

"What color was the fur?" shouted a small kit down front.

"The leg I could see was white, all white, and slim, as I recall." Billy wondered if he remembered clearly; it was so quick and dreamlike. The listening cats stirred and murmured to one another: who was it?

"I bet it was Gretchen," wailed the kit. "She's mostly white like that, with black around her eyes."

Anton remembered. He knew her in passing, thought of her as spunky but naïve. She concentrated so intently while fishing that once he had stood right next to her without her noticing. When he cleared his throat, she startled so severely that she fell in the pool. Anton smiled briefly at the memory.

"Anybody seen her today?" asked the older female, looking around fearfully. Anton recognized her now—her name was Mildred; she was Gretchen's grandmother.

No one had seen Gretchen. The gathering shifted, the older ones shaking their heads, the young ones chattering shrilly.

Old Billy raised his thin voice above the commotion. "Remember, friends, you know what is said." He spoke slowly and many in the crowd nodded gravely. "Where the eye sees the eye, the lost shall be found."

Anton sighed and turned away. He had indeed heard the saying before, but he had no idea what it meant.

⚜ ⚜ ⚜

As he began to join the fishing crews more often, Cecil loved telling Anton his seafaring tales, exaggerating some and drawing them out in the recounting, and Anton grudgingly listened, outwardly skeptical though inwardly curious. Whether drenched and battered in a sudden storm, accidentally trapped in a bait barrel, or nipped painfully by a vicious lobster, Cecil told of his adventures with exuberance. But there was one story that Cecil kept to himself, in part because he thought it might frighten Anton, and in part because even he didn't fully understand what had happened.

Every now and again, when the boat was far from land and the sailors were whiling away the slow hours between duties, someone spotted a great whale swimming a long way off in the sea. The whales often breached the water's surface, slowly rolling like huge logs or surging straight up and splashing thunderously back down. The men knew what kinds of whales they were and pointed and shouted their names: "Humpback!" or "Fin!" or, rarely, "Right one, there!" These whales were closer than any Cecil had seen from the lighthouse, and their enormity intrigued and terrified him.

One sunny day as a thin breeze left the sails slack, Cecil sat on a crate near the starboard railing waiting for the catch to be hauled in. A shout from one of the men drew the others to look over the port side of the ship down at the trawl nets. A large school of cod had swum frantically into the nets from underneath, tugging on the boat with their effort, which was odd. Cecil sat watching, front paws folded under his chest, when out of the corner of his eye he saw a shadow darken the water far out on the starboard side, away from where the crewmen were grouped. He turned, looking for a passing cloud, but the sky was clear. The shadow disappeared, then reappeared much closer, and Cecil realized with a thud in his stomach that it was something dark *in* the water, something as big as the schooner.

Cecil cautiously peered over the side and saw hundreds of small fish scattering in every direction, and then suddenly the shadow was right next to the boat and growing. As he watched, the sea began to spill away from a single spot, smooth and black, expanding down the length of the ship until Cecil understood he was looking at one whole side of a huge finback whale.

The whale made no sound and smelled like the brine of ancient oceans. Its skin was blue-gray with crusty yellow patches, and an immense white jaw wrapped around its wide mouth. Cecil jumped up with his back arched and tail straight as a broom handle, but could not make himself run away. The whale floated gently and Cecil saw its eye, dark blue and big as the round lantern in the lighthouse, passing over the ship, up to the sails and down the tall mast, coming to rest on Cecil.

A pattern of ivory barnacles curved above the eye like a long wizened eyebrow on an old man. The whale's eye surveyed Cecil, as if curiously taking his measure. Cecil was transfixed, and as the eye opened a bit more he felt that the whale was going to tell him a secret, share a piece of wisdom. Cecil felt that he was falling into the depths of that eye and the knowledge that lay behind it, and he held his breath.

"Finny on starboard!" bellowed the captain, almost in Cecil's ear. "All hands to starboard!" he shouted as every fisherman rushed across the deck, their combined weight causing the ship to pitch into the whale with an echoing *thunk*. The whale's eye released Cecil and flickered toward the men. Its powerful tail pushed against the boat, and Cecil nearly tumbled overboard but managed to cling to the crate with his claws. The men were hysterical with fear that the whale would upend the ship. "Drive him off!" some of them screamed. There were no weapons to hand, and in their terror the men began throwing anything available: ropes, boxes, hooks, barrels. These thumped and smashed across the whale's head and broad back. With a final glance at Cecil the whale arched its massive back and dived into the sea, rocking the ship violently in its wake.

For some time afterward the men prayed to the heavens, thanked the stars, told and retold the story of their escape among themselves. They were sure the whale had been an omen, an evil spirit, a test that had been passed. Though the great finback was not seen again that day, every pair of eyes on the ship scanned the ocean for any sign of its return. Only one pair belonged to a creature who actually wished for it.

CHAPTER 3

Brother Cats

The sailors who frequented the saloon had a favorite song, and it was Anton's favorite as well. It had a refrain he waited for, his ears alert, his eyes unblinking, as he gazed through the smoke from his place behind the door. He recognized the words without knowing their meaning. He could run them through his head and pick them out sometimes in the speech of the men on the wharf: "Windy weather boys, stormy weather boys." And then followed by "When the wind blows, we're all together boys." Anton, crouched in his corner, felt his fur lift along his spine.

One chilly night, as the crowd took up this refrain, Anton was so enraptured that he peeked out from his hiding place. He wanted to be part of the music, and he looked at the people in the room for something that might explain to him why he was so drawn to it. How curious these faces were. Why were their noses the same color as their faces? Why was all the fur attached at either end of the head or, in some cases, only one end? Their movements were clumsy, and they made a lot of noise everywhere they went; they could be dangerous, as Sonya had warned, but this singing together brought out something that made Anton feel bold. Unthinking, he stuck his head out a little farther. He could see the singer and a man playing an instrument that whined like a tuneful wind.

Just then the barman shoved the door aside, knocking Anton flat on his back, but only for a moment. Anton surged up, gathering his feet beneath him for a leap past the grumbling man to the top of a barrel. Worse luck, it was the barrel the barman was after and the sight of Anton balanced precariously upon it made him shout.

"Out!" he commanded, waving his hand toward the bar. "Out with you, you sneaking creature."

Anton dived from the barrel, scrambling across the floor into the bar. Two men leaning against the high counter gave a shout of delight as he cleared the edge in one powerful jump. The wood was slippery and Anton skidded against the rail, but as the men made encouraging comments, he recovered his footing and leaped into the bustling room. The women laughed, the men taunted with what they thought were cat sounds. The barman came out and shouted something that made everyone laugh. Anton could see the door just ahead, but it was closed tight against the chill night. Boots were everywhere between him and his destination, and hands reached out to catch him, but he eluded them. The thought that he might be touched by these giant, rough, loud creatures made his throat feel tight. His eyes darted this way and that, and his ears rotated front to back, listening for a sound that would lead him to safety.

And then he heard it, the thudding of boots approaching the door, the squeak of the hinges with a blast of icy air, as two new patrons came bustling inside, eager to get out of the cold. Anton recognized one of them, a young man wearing a bright bandana around his head, a singer with a voice like a summer breeze. Anton regretted that he couldn't stay to listen as he made a dash for the four boots, spotted an opening between an unmatched pair, and shot out into the dark night.

Anton kept running until he made the last turn to the lighthouse path. His brother was there, poking among the rocks near the shore, looking for something to eat. Cecil thrust his paws down between two jagged stones. Anton, wanting to appear casual and calm, slowed to a trot. He approached his brother's tail, which was all he could see of him, waving gaily in the air. "Did you catch something?" he asked.

Cecil's head came up. A small bluish creature struggled between his powerful jaws. "Crab," he said through the helplessly flailing claws.

"Yum," said Anton, who hadn't eaten since morning.

Cecil flung the crab across the rocks, where it landed at his brother's front paws. "You can have him," he said. "My sailors gave me so much fish today, I'm stuffed."

Anton pawed the crab and sunk his teeth into the still soft shell. *My* sailors? he thought. "Thanks," he said.

"Did you see the big ship that came in this morning? It has *four* masts. Billy called it a barque. You can hardly get across the dock for all the crates they took off it. All my sailors were gathered round it like it was a wonder of the world."

Anton pulled off a claw with his teeth and swallowed it whole. "Didn't see it," he mumbled. "I was sleeping."

"It's no way to live the way you're living, brother," Cecil cautioned. "You're in the pub all night and you sleep all day. You're not eating. You'll lose your edge and won't be able to catch your dinner."

Anton finished off the crab and sat licking his whiskers clean. There was no point in arguing with Cecil when he was in his know-it-all mood, but Anton couldn't resist. "A cat who is stuffed with fish all day by sailors can't be called much more than a pet."

"What can I do?" Cecil replied. "I'm not going to turn down a nice piece of mackerel. That would be crazy."

Anton gazed out over the dark water. "Are there any more of these crabs?"

"There's a bunch of them. They're having a party in the rocks."

Anton smiled at the idea of a crab party. "I think I'll go spoil the fun," he said. He stretched his legs and arched his back, limbering up for the sport.

"I'm not a pet," Cecil said.

"They call you by a name," Anton replied. "You'll end up as fat as old Billy at the harbormaster's office; they call him Fletcher. His stomach swings like a bag of clamshells."

"I'm not a pet, I'm a sailor."

"What do they call you?"

"Blackie. Blackjack. Sometimes Lucky Black."

"What does it mean?"

"I have no idea."

Anton raised a paw and extended his claws, then picked at a clot of something between his toes.

"Don't you want to come see the barque?" Cecil asked.

"You know Mother has warned us about those ships. They don't come sailing back every day like the schooners. They go out for months on end. Some never come back again. Promise me you won't go hanging around and get impressed on one of those things."

"They won't be taking cats tonight; they just got here."

"I'm still hungry," Anton said.

"I'll wait for you. It's bigger than a building. It has at least a thousand sails."

Anton chuckled. "A thousand sails," he said.

"Well, a hundred."

"If I go with you to see this ship, will you come listen to the shanties at the saloon? There's a fine singer coming on later tonight. He's there every week."

"It's full of smoke in those places," Cecil complained.

"It's cold on the dock," Anton countered.

"All right, all right," Cecil said. "Eat your crabs and we'll go out for a good time, like two brother sailors."

Anton rolled his shoulders back, did one last head-to-tail stretch. "Like two brother cats," he said as he crept out over the rocks.

⚜ ⚜ ⚜

By the time Anton and Cecil got to the dock, the cargo had been largely cleared away. They discovered it was being loaded onto the ship rather than off. "It must have been empty," Anton observed. "It must be a new ship."

Billy, the harbormaster's cat, came shambling up from alongside the gangplank. "Brand-new, she is," he said, "just out of the yard in Gloucester. She's called the *Mary Anne*. You see that figurehead?"

The brothers regarded the brightly painted figure just under the flying bridge. Two young girls in blue dresses with golden hair and golden shoes held hands and seemed to dance on the air. "That's Mary and Anne, the owner's daughters," Billy said. "He's a shipbuilder himself and this is the biggest vessel ever built on this side."

"This side of what?" Cecil asked.

"The ocean," said Billy pompously. "The great sea."

Cecil bowed his head and allowed the words to flow over him like a wave breaking over a ship's prow. He thought of the whale, its wondrous eye rolling up from the receding waters to look at him, so wise, so at ease in his element, the sea.

"The ocean," Anton growled. "Even this great monster of a boat is no match for that."

"Cats have gone out; a few come back," said Billy solemnly. "There's other lands they say, all sorts of wonders."

"But you've never gone?" Cecil asked.

"I never leave this harbor. Why would I? This is the best life a cat can find in all the wide world and across all the seas. Those as come back say it's so."

"That's what Mother says," Anton agreed.

"Well, she's right," said Billy. "Best be off home now. Dangerous out here this time of night, as you boys well know." He cast them a sidelong look and waddled off, his belly rolling from side to side like a seaman's hammock in a storm.

Anton looked up at the soaring masts of the big ship, with its crossbars on all four, the square sails rolled up tight and the dark basket of the crow's nest brooding atop the mizzenmast. Up and down the gangplank the sailors made their way, bandy-legged and crouched beneath the heavy crates and barrels, all bound, he thought, for where? A place like here? Or a land made entirely of sand? Or one where the humans had fur and swung from the trees? Too frightening even to imagine.

"It's a grand ship," Cecil said. "When I look at a ship like this, I can't deny I'd like to see where they go."

"Don't think about it," Anton cautioned. "Come

and hear the singing and you'll never want to leave again."

Somewhere nearby they heard the snap of a dry twig, or it could have been the crackle of a torch, or the creak of a stacked barrel. Whatever it was, in an instant the brothers vanished, and they didn't stop running until they reached the town.

CHAPTER 4

Impressment

Why is it, Anton wondered, that when you've been to a place you love, and you try to share it with a friend, it's suddenly a different place?

Anton slipped into the saloon storeroom quickly, scarcely ruffling his smooth gray fur. Cecil got his big head through the opening but then he was stuck. "It's fine," he said. "I can hear quite well from here."

"But you can squeeze in if you try," Anton urged him. "Just push in one shoulder at a time."

"Easy for you to say; you're as slim as an eel."

"Just try. I'm sure you can squeeze in."

Cecil pulled his head out, and for a moment, Anton thought he had given up, but then one white paw came through the narrow space, followed by a black shoulder. Then Cecil's head, pressed tight against the other shoulder, shoved through. "Now you've got it," Anton encouraged him. The back half of Cecil glided in. He sat up, looking dazed.

"I squashed my head," he said, passing a paw over one ear. "This had better be good."

The door was pushed to the wall with a barrel holding it in place so there was nothing to hide behind—not that anyone was looking into the store-room. Two sailors were shouting at each other at one table and a woman was weeping at another while the bartender went up and down, muttering to his patrons as he filled their glasses. The brothers looked in, Anton dismayed and Cecil frankly disdainful. "Wow, I love that tune," Cecil said.

Anton shot him a pained look. "They haven't started yet."

Cecil's ears rotated front to back and he stretched his neck up, taking a slow breath. "There's a mouse in here."

"Ugh," said Anton.

"It would give us something to do while we wait for the fabulous singing."

"It would bring the barman on our tails," Anton replied. "He's not a kindly one."

One of the shouting men rose from his table and threw his mug at the other sailor. The mug hit the floor and rolled into the storeroom. Cecil turned toward the loose board.

"That does it for me," he said. "I'm sleepy. I want to be up and out on the water early. If you want to see what it is they sing about, you should join me." And with that he nudged the board aside and, after a brief struggle, disappeared into the night.

Anton felt his spirits flag as his brother's fluffy tail slipped away. He'd pictured Cecil swaying along with the music, admitting that it was better than he'd imagined it would be, but now he was gone. And of course in the next moment the stringed instrument let out a mournful wail and the singer launched into a ballad Anton recognized, as sad as it was sweet. He lay down by the barrel and curled himself into a ball, letting the music comfort him.

✤ ✤ ✤

When Anton woke, the room was quiet. The whole saloon was dark, the barman was gone, and not a sailor in the place. A thin, milky light streamed in through the opaque glass in the front door. All the chairs were turned upside down on the tables, and there was a strong smell of vinegar in the air. Anton yawned and stretched, feeling foolish. How had he slept through the night without anyone noticing he was there? He crawled out through the opening and stood in the alley. The air was fresh and briny, and the light was so soft it looked as if the shops lining the dirt road had been painted with a pink brush. Anton took a deep breath, thinking again of his brother. Cecil's parting words came back to him. He was out there on the wharf right now, no doubt, waiting for the fishermen to come clambering up the gangplank, calling him "lucky" and welcoming him aboard. "If you want to see what it is they sing about," Cecil had said, "you should join me."

Anton darted through an alley at the end of the lane and came out on the wharf near the harbormaster's office. Billy was there, purring heavily as he lapped at a bowl of milk his master had left for him. He sat back as Anton approached, running his tongue around his lips, pulling in the last drops. "Good morning," Anton said.

"You're up early," Billy observed.

"I fell asleep in the saloon," Anton admitted. "I'm on my way home."

"Even your brother's not out yet, and he's the earliest cat on the docks."

The office door opened and the harbormaster stepped out in conversation with a ship's officer. Anton and Billy were silent as the two men walked past, heading toward the great barque, the *Mary Anne,* which now rested low at anchor, its gangplank nearly flush with the dock.

"That's the captain of the new ship," Billy informed Anton. "She sails this morning. Let's walk down and watch her cast off."

Anton agreed, though he found Billy's insistence on calling ships "she" a bit ridiculous, coming from a cat. A light rain began to fall as they followed the men to the ship, where the sailors shimmied up and down, tightening lines and checking the rigging on sails, busy as bees in a swarm around the queen. The captain was greeted by two officers standing at the top of the gangplank. As they spoke the men and the two cats all observed a disturbing sight. A large brown rat scurried out from under the dock, leaped onto a line, and rushed up and out of sight through a porthole.

"Curse the creature," the captain said. "My beautiful, clean new ship doesn't need a cargo of those devils."

"You'll need a feline," the harbormaster observed. "They leave a boat in droves if they know there's a cat on board."

"True enough," said the captain. "Where will I find myself such a creature?"

Anton and Billy stood looking on, absorbed in their own observations. "They've got a rat on already," Billy said. "And probably not the first or the last."

Anton shuddered. "I can't bear rats," he said.

"I ate one once," Billy said. "Before I found the harbormaster. Not a tasty meal, but it was better than starving."

"I think I'd rather starve," said Anton.

Turning around, the captain spied the two cats. "I'll be jiggered. There's a pair of them right here."

"You don't want old Fletcher," the harbormaster said. "He's too lazy and he lives on cream."

"What are they up to?" Billy said, voicing a

suspicion Anton apprehended a moment too late. Suddenly the harbormaster reached down, grabbed Anton by the scruff of his neck, and whipped him high into the air.

"Here he is, I've got one for you," said the harbormaster.

Anton popped out all his claws and battled the air with his legs, but he couldn't reach anything, hanging as he was like a kitten in his mother's jaws. What was going on? Cats didn't get impressed in the light of day. It was a dark-night business, shameful and cruel. The sailor came up and Anton tried to sink a claw into him, but the sailor grasped Anton's paws from behind and held them together while gripping his neck flesh tightly as the harbormaster handed him over.

"Look," said the sailor. "He's a fierce fellow." Then he was off, up the gangplank, holding the flailing Anton out before him like a squirming fish. On the deck the sailors laughed at his struggles and one said, "It was like that for me, brother. I didn't want to go to sea." At last Anton understood his efforts were to no avail; the grip on his neck only tightened as he fought. He let himself hang loosely and raised his eyes, looking out across the deck where the ships were lined up, the wharf busy now with sailors moving to and fro. Down past the fishing schooners Anton saw a sight that made him cry aloud. Cecil was striding purposefully around the bend from the lighthouse path.

"Cecil!" Anton called. "Cecil, they're taking me away!"

"Put him in the hold until we're off," said the captain. A sailor stepped forward and yanked up a plank door, beneath which loomed a ladder and a black hole. Anton wriggled and strained to see down the dock. He glimpsed Cecil bounding past Billy and breaking into a gallop toward the *Mary Anne.*

"In you go," the man clutching Anton said. "You're a sailor now." He took a step down into the hold, dangled Anton out as far from the ladder as he could, and dropped him all at once into the darkness below.

✣ ✣ ✣

After his adventures with Anton at the saloon the night before, it was well past dawn when Cecil trotted down the path from the lighthouse. The sharp smell of approaching rain hung in the air. "Out too late, slept in too long," he muttered, hoping he hadn't already missed his fishing schooner. Anton had been unenthusiastic about the big ship last night, almost dismissive. Miffed, Cecil resolved not to bother trying to convert Anton any further. *Nope, not a drop of sailor blood in that cat, that's for sure,* he thought.

Rounding the corner of the harbormaster's house, Cecil squinted down the long row of ship bows tied to the piers along the dock. His heart sank. The schooner had gone out, and to make matters even less pleasant, a misting rain began. The big barque was still in, however, with a great deal of activity around her, sailors swinging across the masts unfurling the sails, and more crew criss-crossing the decks with crates and boxes. Cecil sat under the eaves of the house and watched, envious and morose. Where was she bound, and what would she do there? He could just make out the figurehead of the two young girls, a little silly for such a majestic ship, in his opinion. Better would be a wild animal like those their mother had told stories of, or even a cat, a really dignified cat.

Suddenly a real cat flashed into view, hustling down the dock toward him. It was Billy, his stubby legs propelling his sloshing girth as fast as they could manage. "Cecil!" he huffed, gasping to catch his breath. "Anton!" he panted.

"I have no idea where Anton is. He didn't come home . . ." began Cecil.

"The *Mary Anne*!" Billy struggled with the words.

"Quite a ship, yes . . ."

"They took Anton!" Billy finally expelled with effort.

"*Took* him? Oh, *no*," Cecil moaned as he hurtled past Billy and down the wharf.

"Casting off!" Cecil heard Billy yell behind him and his heart jumped higher in his chest. The dock boards were slippery in the fine rain, and Cecil dodged legs, bales, and netting as he plunged toward the barque. The ship was set sideways against the pier, with the gangplank stretched across nearer the aft end. He could see the men's hands grasping the edge of the plank, lifting it off the ship's rail.

Anton, where are you? Where did they put you? Cecil thought desperately. Careening down the pier he prepared to dash across the plank but the men had pulled it swiftly onto the ship's deck, and Cecil saw with horror at the last moment that the

jump was too wide. Jamming to a halt at the edge of the pier with an angry yowl, he looked around wildly for another way on.

Men on the piers were pulling the thick, heavy ropes up over the wide posts and tossing them up to the deck. One rope had been cast away, and the ship drifted closer to the pier where the remaining rope held. Cecil streaked to the end of the pier to reach the ship's fore. The new timbers creaked and rattled; the barque seemed almost eager to be unbound from land. The dockhands struggled with the last loops of rope and heaved them up to the deck, where they uncoiled and hung halfway down the side, and the great ship slowly began to draw away. Cecil gathered all his strength and sprang from the dock out over the water, catching the end of one hanging rope in his claws, whumping cruelly into the broad side of the boat but still hanging on. The dockhands hooted in amazement watching the frantic cat. *I made it!* Cecil thought for a brief moment, but the rope was slick with rain and his claws shredded the fraying threads. *Splunk.* He dropped like a rock into the cold water below.

Spluttering and gasping for breath, legs thrashing

to stay afloat, Cecil peered up at the towering side of the barque sliding steadily away from him. The girls in the blue dresses surged ahead, their angelic faces turned toward the harbor and the waiting ocean. The water churned and swirled around him in the ship's wake. Cecil weakened and his body went slack, the reality like a lead weight in the pit of his stomach. He *hadn't* saved Anton, not even close! Now he found himself sinking, choking on the water filling his nose and eyes. He felt as if a heavy net had closed over him and was dragging him down; he could not move his limbs. Was this what drowning felt like?

Then abruptly he was lifted into the air, flying swiftly over the water and landing in a sodden heap on the dock. He coughed out seawater and opened his eyes to see Ben holding a long wooden pole attached to the small basket of netting in which Cecil was now slumped. Ben dropped the pole and rushed over.

"Blackie my lad! Are ya all right there? What's got into ya, jumpin' in the harbor like that?" He knelt down and smoothed Cecil's fur with his rough hands, looking at him anxiously.

Cecil found his breath at last and stood up

shakily. The dockhands watched with amusement, not sure what to make of his strange antics. Cecil gazed at Ben with what he hoped was a look of gratitude, though his head was full of numb fear, then slunk quietly away from the staring sailors. As he stumbled up the wharf in the steady rain, shivering with cold and despair, he could see the tops of the *Mary Anne*'s masts in the distance, already sailing through the mouth of the harbor and out to sea, headed for parts unknown. His brother was aboard, and Cecil was left behind, wet and miserable on the dock.

CHAPTER 5

On the *Mary Anne*

own, down into the vast dark hold of the ship Anton fell. He braced his legs for landing, but when it came, his hind paws missed the edge of a barrel and he hung by his claws, seeking purchase on the rough staves of the side. In a moment he'd pulled himself up and sat atop the barrel, cautiously wrapping his tail around his legs. His ears rotated, taking in a hubbub of sounds. His eyes, gradually adjusting to the dark, made out shapes and calculated distances. He looked up at the thin, bright lines of light framing the door of the hold high over his head.

The ladder was nearly vertical, the rungs far apart. It wouldn't be easy to climb. Noises came from the deck, men shouting and stamping their many boots, dragging gear and reeling in ropes, hauling up the gangplank, scrambling up the masts. From below there was another sound, soft and insistent, the throb of water rubbing lazily against the wood of the hull, feeling it over for cracks, for a way in.

Anton's brain worked over his predicament. The hold was crammed with barrels, but along one wall wooden crates were stacked, some so high they nearly touched the ceiling. He could still hear the shouting, though the voices seemed farther away now. The churning of the water rushing back from the moving prow grew louder until it drowned out all other sound. Anton's heart thumped with terror; they had cast off—the ship was setting out to sea.

Abruptly the hold shifted. The crates rattled against the wall and the barrels banged together, throwing Anton off balance. He had seen Cecil coming up the dock, and he knew Billy would have told him what had happened. He also knew that with all the noise of sea and men, no one would hear a cat calling out in the darkness at the bottom of the hold, but he couldn't help himself. He dug all his claws into the wooden lid of the barrel, lifted his head, and howled, "Cecil, Cecil! Where are you?"

But the only reply came from the water slapping against the hull as the great ship pulled away from the wharf and the sailors unfurled the sails with joyful shouts. *How fine,* Anton thought, *to watch a ship sail away from the wharf and how different to be trapped inside it.* He closed his eyes and swallowed; his mouth was dry and his stomach felt queasy. Soon, he persuaded himself, they would open the hold and somehow he'd get up that ladder and into the light. He peered up the wall of crates again and a new thought occurred to him. Carefully he began to climb, jumping lightly from one offset edge to the next, testing his weight on each level. Close to the top he could go no farther, but now he was only a couple of yards from the door.

His jaws stretched wide in a yawn. The great defense for all cats in times of stress is sleep, and so sleep crept up on Anton and seized him as he tried to think of what to do next. He slipped into a dream of home. He was a kitten, lounging on the blanket with Cecil and Sonya in the old lighthouse, savoring the smell of salt and herrings, beneath glittering stars.

A crack like a thunderbolt shattered this blissful dream, and Anton opened his eyes to a widening swath of golden light glaring from above. Before the sailors had the door wide enough to look inside, he was up the ladder and out between their legs, bolting across the deck in search of a hiding place. He spotted a coil of rope and dived into the center of it. Then he crouched down, listening for sounds of pursuit, but only the wind passed over his head as the sun warmed the hemp near his face. He sniffed the air, laden with unfamiliar scents. Where there were men, there was food, he thought, and sooner or later the men would go to bed.

Anton looked up at the great sails, a dozen or more of them bloated by the wind, attended by sailors who balanced on spars and hung from ropes, dwarfed by the size and power of the enormous canvases they somehow contrived to control. Anton stuck his head out, looking across the deck at a group of sailors gathered beneath the main mast, and another two standing in the open door of the cabin. They looked cheerful; they laughed and jostled each other and pointed at the ocean. *I'm at sea,* Anton thought. *This is where Cecil wants to be.* The ship forged through the waves, pitching from side to side. A wave splashed over the rail and soaked him from head to tail. Anton wiped his face with his paw, tasting the salty water as he licked his pad to smooth his whiskers. *And I just want to be home,* he thought.

The two men near the cabin moved away, and Anton could see into the open doorway. It would be dry in there; perhaps he would find something to eat. He studied the space in between—a good dash and he'd be inside before any of the sailors could catch him. Gathering his strength, he eased down the side of the coil and then ran full out, his paws scarcely touching the planks of the deck, ignoring the shout from one sailor and the raucous laughter of another, until he was in the cabin. At once he spotted another open door and made for it. Here, to his surprise, was a narrow hall with doors on each side. *Hide, hide,* he thought. *There must be a place.* The last door opened into a small room crammed with canvas bags, the rafters strung with long white planks that smelled like fish.

Anton spied a space between two bags and squeezed into it. On either side, other bags leaned together, making a dome over an oblong bit of floor. It was just big enough for a cat. He curled himself in a ball and rested his head on his paws. There were many strange smells in the place. Some he had not encountered before, but there was an insistent, sour, greasy odor he recognized, and it made him wrinkle his nose with distaste. He had no doubt what it was. He was sharing lodgings with a rat.

Again Anton slept. He woke, hungry and thirsty and uncertain where he was. There was a noise and then another, a sailor's voice and the scrape of something heavy being dragged into the passageway. He sat up and peered through an opening between the bags. Two sailors were talking and laughing. One was pointing out things in the room to the other. Before Anton could make a move, the bigger of the two men shifted a bag and Anton was exposed to their view.

"Well, you're in the right place, lad," the big sailor said.

"Though he won't find much to his taste in the larder," observed the other.

Anton looked from one to the other as they spoke, though he had no idea what they were saying.

"He's a bit of a scrawny fellow, idn't he?" said the first.

"There's not much meat upon him," his companion agreed.

The big sailor leaned forward and crooked his finger at Anton. "Come along, mate, and we'll introduce you to Pritchert. He's the cook. He'll be your benefactor."

Why were they talking to him in this pointless way? Anton wondered. And what was the meaning of the crooked finger? Now the other sailor joined in, motioning toward the doorway with his palm. "Come along, then," he said. They backed out into the hall, urging Anton with their gestures. They didn't seem threatening, and if he was to get anything to eat he knew it would have to come from them. He thought of the sailors who stuffed Cecil with fish because they thought he was lucky. Anton stood up, stretched from head to tail, ran a quick paw over his face, and followed the men into a room with a long table, where a third sailor stood over a barrel, dipping a tin can on a string into an opening in the lid.

Water was in that barrel. Anton could smell it, and he was so thirsty he forgot his sense of ordinary caution and leaped onto the lid, thrusting his face close to the opening, which caused the sailors to laugh.

"Water, water everywhere, and not a drop to drink, eh, mate?" said the sailor pulling up the can. He was a tall, thin, white-haired fellow with a beard that stood out from his face like a cloud passing by. "Hand me that pie pan," he added to the sailor nearest him, who took down a tin plate from a stack over the stove. The cloudy man had pulled up the can and proceeded to pour the contents into the plate. Anton lapped at the cool water, oblivious to danger. When his tongue had chased out every last drop, he sat up, licking his whiskers. The three men stood looking at him, their eyes bright with amusement.

"What name shall we give our feline friend?" said one.

"Thirsty," suggested the other.

Sailors, Anton thought. They all looked alike,

but it might be a good idea to tell them apart. The fur was the thing; some had a lot and some had hardly any. He would have to be observant and figure out which was which. He'd call the white-bearded one "Cloudy," and the thin fellow, who had no fur on his chin but a great mop of black fur falling over his eyes, he would call "Black Top."

"He's not got a spot of color on him. Let's call him Mr. Gray," the first sailor said. And so they did.

❖ ❖ ❖

Two more days passed and Anton tried to make some sort of life below decks, avoiding the chilly spray and endlessly pitching deck at all costs. The noxious smell of the rat irritated him, but he had not spied the creature yet. Anton slept in the galley, because it was quiet there, and crept about, waiting until Cloudy was alone to present himself for a daily pan of water. When the men had their dinner, they were rowdy and Anton stayed outside the door, sniffing the air. The food they ate had no appeal for him. It was some sort of biscuit and potatoes and nasty-smelling soup. The sailors were hungry and cleaned their plates, not thinking to offer Anton a taste. When Cloudy was clearing up, he scraped the pots into a plate and offered it to Anton. It was all he could do to choke down a bite or two.

"You'll get used to it, lad," Cloudy said, but Anton was thinking, *How am I going to survive?*

Then, early one morning, when the sailors were still snoring in their bunks and the night watchman was taking a last turn around the deck, Cloudy went into the larder to fill a big tin box with flour from a bag, and Anton followed. Cat and man heard a rustle and pricked up their ears. Anton knew immediately what it was, but Cloudy evidently did not. In the next moment a large brown rat stepped out from behind a barrel. Cloudy gave a shout and dropped his tin, backing clumsily into the hall, his beard aquiver and his eyes staring wildly.

"Be gone, you devilish creature!" he cried.

The rat turned calmly away and slipped back into its hiding place, its long tail disappearing bit by bit. It paused to wheeze, looking back over its shoulder. "This is my ship, you lousy cat," it said. "You'd best make yourself scarce."

Anton shuddered. It was one thing to smell the creature, but to see the ugly snout and beady eyes, the sharp claws and slithering tail, turned his stomach. No cat, not even Cecil, relished the prospect of a battle with a large rat.

Cloudy charged back into the room, taking up his tin, and to Anton's surprise, shook it at him, shouting in outrage, "What are you up to, you lazy, worthless fellow? It's your job to clear the ship of vermin!" Anton had no idea why the man was upset, but clearly he was angry, and clearly he was angry at Anton. He filled the tin with flour and huffed off to the galley, leaving Anton in a miserable state of mind.

Anton slipped into the galley after the sailors finished their morning gruel, thinking he might be able to get a bite of something, but Cloudy spotted him and waved him out of the room, berating him, as he had before. The sailors listened, frowned, muttered, and turned unfriendly faces on Anton.

"Get on with you then," Black Top hissed, pointing to the storeroom with a gnarled finger. "Do your duty like the rest of us."

Anton was hungry; he'd been hungry for days. Was Cloudy now going to deny him even the tasteless stuff he'd been living on thus far? He was indeed. At lunch and then at dinner, the sailors

treated Anton coldly. When Cloudy scraped the pans at the end of the meal, he stepped out onto the deck and threw the contents of the tin plate over the side. Anton had followed him and his stomach twisted and groaned as he watched the gray mess fly over the rail. What was he going to do?

CHAPTER 6

Racing the Storm

or several long minutes, Sonya sat looking out through a slit in the lighthouse wall. She shook her head and slowly turned back to Cecil. Her elegant face was pained and drawn, though her eyes were bright in the dim light.

"You've got to go find him and bring him home," she said softly.

Cecil gulped. He was terrified for his brother, but here was Cecil's chance to sail the open seas. "Will you come with me?" he asked.

"I have new kittens to take care of; I can't leave them alone. You must go."

Cecil hung his head. "Ma, I'm so sorry, it's my fault . . ."

Sonya waved a paw and began to pace, speaking more quickly. "Did you talk to Billy? What did he say?" she asked.

Cecil straightened up. He *had* at least thought to do this. "He said that since the ship was so big, with so much cargo aboard"—Cecil fought the panic in his voice—"she probably wasn't coming back, not for a long while at least."

Sonya squeezed her eyes shut for a moment. "That sounds right. He's seen these things." She pulled herself up and took a breath, stepping quickly over to Cecil and looking directly into his eyes. "Listen, now, you must be strong. Get Billy's help. Choose a ship, and follow as best you can." She touched his nose briefly with her own.

Cecil looked down and fidgeted with a loose stone, thinking of his brother. "He doesn't even *like* sailing."

"I know." Sonya sighed.

"He's not very brave, either."

"He may surprise you."

❧ ❧ ❧

For three agonizing days, Cecil watched every ship entering the harbor, waiting for one different from the smaller fishing schooners he knew did not travel far. At first he thought he'd wait for another just like Anton's, but Billy advised against it.

"Not many like that one, an original she was," Billy said, rubbing a paw thoughtfully under his chin. "Your best bet is to look for something big, plain and simple."

On the evening of the third day after Anton was impressed, a tall square-rigged clipper sped into the harbor and pivoted to dock with a flourish. She was sleek and long, flying flags of red and green and displaying a figurehead of a bull with sharp curved horns and a ring through its nose. The crew had tanned skin and dark eyes. The captain's shirt was trimmed with ruffled fabric at the wrists and chest, and golden threads glittered in his headscarf. The sailors unloaded their cargo briskly and moved out to the saloon, leaving a few of the younger men behind to load crate after crate of salted fish up to the deck. No one noticed a black creature, blending with the deepening night sky, as it crept silently up the plank, slipped between the weathered barrels, and disappeared.

※ ※ ※

Cecil waited out the night in his hiding place in the storage area below decks, wedged in a dark and smelly corner behind three heavy barrels. No sooner did he begin to hear activity on the deck above him than the ship shivered as it was unmoored. The clipper cast off as it had come in, arcing theatrically away from the piers and bursting through the mists of the gray dawn out to the harbor and the waiting sea. Cecil guessed that they were probably going quite a bit faster than the old schooners, but his growing hunger quickly pushed these thoughts aside. He realized he had not eaten much since he last saw Anton—*oh!* the thought of poor Anton made his head throb with worry—and his stomach was snarling.

Hours passed as the day wore on, and when he could stand neither the suspense nor the confines any longer, he considered trying to slip out of the storage area to see what was going on. Most likely the men would be happy about a cat on board, but there was always the risk they would simply throw him over the side as a nuisance. Cecil squirmed in his hiding place. It wouldn't do Anton any good if his rescuer starved to death, he reasoned. Listening intently for any movement nearby, Cecil clawed up and over the top of the wall of barrels and looked around in the gloom, his nose working furiously.

The small room was completely stuffed with barrels, most of which smelled of fish. Another strong scent Cecil couldn't place floated on top of that. He launched himself forward, thumping across the barrelheads from one to the next, closing in on a particular fishiness. Finally he squeezed his girth down between barrels to the grimy floor, where he found one cracked slat that revealed the barrel's contents. Fish! Eagerly he clawed at a bit of exposed pale meat until a fat, stiff chunk fell out in front of him, and he gobbled it ravenously.

Just as he swallowed the last bit he realized that the strong odor he had noticed was not coming from something separate in the hold but was actually *part* of the fish, and he began to gag. *What kind of fish is this?* he thought with disgust. *It tastes like pure salt.* He pawed at his tongue to get the horrid stuff off, then felt his throat seize up, and he sank to the floor. Splayed out between barrels, lips puckering, tongue lolling, eyes watering, Cecil had just one thought: *Water!*

The door creaked open, spilling in gray light and wet spray. Cecil pressed his bulk weakly against a barrel bottom, trying not to be seen. No one came in, however, and the spray continued. He blinked up into the dull sky and dimly perceived that it must be raining, though it wasn't doing him any good where he was. He resolved to drag himself to the top of the barrel to get a better view. Once on top, though, his stomach revolted over its contents and he collapsed in a sick heap just as he heard voices from men entering the room.

"Look there, it's a cat," one shouted, then snorted. "A black cat, eh? That's something."

In a haze Cecil was roughly snatched up and carried at arm's length, hanging limp, up to the deck where he was waved around in the air.

"It's dead, no?" asked a deep voice, and the man holding Cecil grunted in agreement. Cecil cracked open one swollen eye to see a tall man with a glittering red headscarf glaring at him distrustfully.

"Get rid of it!" he commanded, pointing over the side of the ship.

Now hold on just a minute, thought Cecil. *Why is he pointing out* there *while apparently discussing* me*?*

As the man holding him strode to the railing, Cecil desperately summoned his voice and let out a strangled yowl, whereupon the man dropped him straightaway to the wet deck with a splat, while the other crewmen hooted in surprise. A low spot in the boards nearby had collected a puddle of rainwater and Cecil rolled onto his paws and dragged himself over to it, lapping up the cool drink. It soothed his throat and his twisted insides. As he crouched on the deck he peered warily at the commanding man, who still scowled with his hands on his hips.

"Capitano!" shouted a sailor hanging from the mast high above. "Storm coming, out of the north!" and all looked in the direction he pointed. Cecil rose up on his haunches to look, too, but saw neither another ship nor land on the horizon as he expected, only a mass of heavy dark clouds. In an instant the mood of the men turned grim. The captain began striding up and down the deck, calling out short bursts of orders punctuated by finger-jabbing in all directions. Sailors scattered

to trim the sails, secure the ropes, and stow loose barrels and crates below. The light rain had turned to a steady shower, and the waves kicking up were not helping Cecil's stomach, but he was grateful to have been forgotten in the commotion.

Cecil crept along the planks, careful to stay out of the way, slurping up any water he found. A stream of blueberries dribbled out of the broken corner of a crate wedged under the deck rail on the port side. A crewman grabbed the crate and stomped away, leaving Cecil to chase the rolling blueberries across the deck as the ship tilted in the waves. He managed to capture most of them and began to feel a little better, only to realize that he'd better find a way back below to avoid the rain while he still had the chance. Too late—the hatch was shut, and the men had closed the doors to their quarters as well. Cecil's fur was soaked, though he didn't mind that as much as the bite of the wind, which had picked up to a low howl. He skittered around the ship looking for shelter and finally tucked himself among some tangled rope under a bundle of canvas tarp. It was not entirely dry and the tarp flapped loudly in the wind, but at least he was mostly out of the rain.

The crew barked at one another as they hurried about their tasks. Cecil watched them scurrying. He had been in a few small squalls on the fishing schooner, but nothing compared to the rapidly blackening sky and intense wind here. The waves were cresting high enough to be seen over the top of the railing, rolling the ship along their deep curves.

"Faster!" the captain roared. Two men strained to set the spanker sail as two more hauled on the mainsail ropes to lock it in place. They all struggled to hold the rigging steady as the wind blasted the sail open wide. Cecil felt the ship rush forward, driven over the ragged waves by the stormy gale. The group of sailors moved aft, shortening the gallant sails to prevent the storm from snapping the mast. *They're trying to outrun it,* Cecil thought, and peeked out farther from his tarp. Fur soaked, wind whistling through his whiskers, he had never in his life moved so fast and his heart thumped with the thrill.

Rain swept over the deck in sheets. Off the starboard side, through the veil of clouded air, Cecil noticed an oddly shaped wave curl past. He swiped a paw past his eyes and looked again. Two waves

side by side popped up and disappeared, but these were moving smoothly *toward* the front of the ship, unlike the rest, which splashed up and fell back. Cecil was sure they were darker and more pointed than usual . . . like fins. He started, then crouched down again, torn between curiosity and a desire to stay out of the lashing rain. He hesitated. But he had to find out!

Cecil clambered across the slippery planks to the rail. Clutching a coil of rope with his claws, he stretched his neck until he could see out into the violently churning sea. A muted warbling, coming from under the water, vibrated in his swiveling ears. As he peered over the side of the swaying ship, two large figures burst from the waves. Cecil flattened himself against the ropes and stared as what looked like miniature whales soared past his eyes in a slow-motion arc and then sliced through the sea with powerful strokes, surging and leaping again. *Wow!* he thought. *What a ride that would be.*

As long as ten cats set nose to tail, with smooth blue-gray skin and covered with speckles, the creatures had curved fins on their backs and smaller flippers on each side. Strong tails propelled them through the water, and a round opening on top of their heads spouted misty air, just as the whale had. Cecil remembered Sonya telling him about dolphins, lightning-fast swimmers who loved to dance in the waves, reputed to be wise and worldly, though nobody he knew had ever seen one up close as none came into the ports. The creatures were keeping pace with the ship, pulling ahead or diving and resurfacing with renewed vigor. They snorted and bobbed their heads, and Cecil had the feeling they were enjoying themselves. With a lurch of the ship the figure nearest to him turned its shiny eyes, black flecked with silver, on the wet cat.

"Mmmmph!" it exhaled in high-pitched surprise, opening its sparkling eyes wider, then turned to its companion. "Adrianna, look over here at the cat creature!" Its voice was squeaky and strange, like watery music. The second figure swam forward to see past the first, then let out a tuneful giggle and waved a flipper.

"Hello, cat creature! You look like a wet rag, I'm afraid!" She laughed, like raindrops drumming on glass, and dived into the waves. Both dolphins had long noses and wide mouths that seemed to be perpetually smiling, or perhaps smirking, at Cecil.

Cecil raised himself up. "Excuse me, who *are*

you?" he shouted through the wind. "What are you doing here?"

The first dolphin turned to him and blasted air from his head in amusement, all the while swimming strongly alongside the speeding ship without appearing to tire.

"I am Leonardo," he said, his liquid voice dropping to a lower pitch and slowing down, as if speaking to a young or dim-witted creature, "and we call ourselves the Maculato. We are without doubt the fastest dolphins in the ocean." He glanced up at Cecil for effect, then continued. "We like to race the ships, you see, but it is only fair to race in a storm such as this. Otherwise we win much too easily." He gestured backward with his great long snout, and Cecil looked down the side toward the stern. He spied eight or nine other similar creatures of different sizes and speckled patterns, veering and bounding crazily in the ship's wake. Adrianna shot up out of the water nearby, executing a perfect backflip and sprinting through the waves to catch up.

"Yes, of course," Cecil called down, though he had never heard of any of this. "You look a bit like whales, you know," he added.

Leonardo let out a disdainful poof of air. "But we are not! No, the whales are much too serious. They are always busy working, never stopping to play. They only leap occasionally—"

"And awkwardly," Adrianna put in.

"And they move so slowly that their skin grows barnacles, like a ship." Leonardo shook his head, still smiling. "We prefer the fun life, excitement, seeing the world."

Adrianna lifted her eyes to the stormy sky and squeaked, "I have heard the mermaids singing, each to each." Cecil, surprised, began to ask about the mermaids, but Leonardo cut in.

"Are you a prisoner?" he called to Cecil, tacking sharply away to avoid being sideswiped by the bucking ship.

Cecil thought about this. "Not really," he shouted. "I'm looking for my brother. Have you seen a gray cat, smaller than me, recently?" He struggled to stay on the ropes as an enormous wave crashed over the railing, drenching him further.

Leonardo shook his long snout briskly. "We don't often see cat creatures in the storms. You are unusual."

Adrianna chuckled again, and chirped to no

one in particular, "This above all: to thine own self be true."

"Right you are! Most wise," said Leonardo, nodding vigorously. He glanced up at Cecil. "She's always got a saying for the occasion. It's quite extraordinary."

Adrianna was surging ahead toward the bow wake when she pulled up as if remembering something. She slowed until she drew even with Leonardo again and smiled up at Cecil, trilling in a high key, like a prophecy, "Where the eye sees the eye." She zigzagged in the waves and began pulling away.

The words rolled around in Cecil's mind like a whirling school of fish. "What does that one mean?" he shouted. He could see that Leonardo was losing interest in him and keen on catching up with his competitor.

"It is where lost things are found. You must go where the eye sees the eye," explained Leonardo. "But I cannot tell you where that is, precisely."

At that moment, a bolt of lightning stabbed the sea close by, flashing in the deep black eyes of the dolphins. They whistled a piercing cry and reared up, all together, then plunged under the waves. They were gone in an instant. Cecil was left, soaked and freezing, alone at the rail.

As he tried to stand on his stiffened legs and unclench his petrified claws, Cecil marveled at the strange beauty of the dolphins, and pondered the saying, "Where the eye sees the eye." Sure, he had heard the crazy phrase from some of the older cats back home but never thought it meant anything, at least not for him. *Where could such a place be?* he thought doubtfully. *And if I found it, would Anton be there for me?*

Darkness was gathering about the ship. Cecil had never been out on the sea at night, though he had long dreamed of it. In his dreams the sky was bright with stars and a pale full moon, their reflections rippling in a tranquil ocean. This was much different; angry waves pitched the ship callously about and thick clouds crowded the night sky. For the first time, Cecil felt horribly alone. *What am I doing?* he asked himself bleakly. *I'll never find Anton in a sea so immense as this.* He wondered how he would even find his way home again.

As he struggled back to his meager shelter, Cecil looked over his shoulder once more, searching for the dolphins frolicking in the storm, but the light was failing and he strained to see through the driving rain. One last flash of bright lightning accompanied by a terrible thunderous boom illuminated the wide, boiling ocean for a long second. Cecil's heart shivered in his chest as he glimpsed, far away but clearly outlined, the immense barnacled tail of a whale slowly disappearing into the deep.

CHAPTER 7

Teeth and Claws

On board the *Mary Anne*, Anton slunk along the hall and into the storeroom, puzzling over the sudden change in his status. It had something to do with the rat. The sailors were as repelled by the creature as he was, and they seemed to hold him responsible. He recalled Billy's story about the time he'd been so hungry he'd been forced to eat one. *Never,* Anton thought, *would I take a bite of such a malodorous creature.* He didn't like sleeping on the same ship with a rat, but he had assumed it would stay out of sight. Why had that big fellow shown his ugly face? Anton sat

84

looking at the flour sacks. He heard a soft scratching against the floor, but there were so many sacks and barrels and crates lining the walls he couldn't see anything.

Then a rasping voice floated up, poisoning the air. "I warned you, but you're still here, you stupid cat. I'll have to get rid of you myself"—a low chuckle—"when you least expect it."

Anton stood and paced in the small room, his brain working over the problem. He was determined to do something, to make his way in this confusing world of sailors and seas and rats. He sat down and gave his face a thorough cleaning. As he flattened his ears and smoothed his cheeks, a resolution came upon him: he would have to kill the rat.

And he would do it at once. He lifted his head and sniffed the air, rotating his ears from front to back, slitting his eyes while he listened and listened, and then he knew exactly where his prey was and how to get to him. He pushed his way between two bags, leaped upon a crate, then walked across a barrel and another crate. At the far edge of the crate he stopped, stretched his neck out, and looked down. And there it was, the snout twitching ceaselessly and the beady eyes peering up into the darkness, where the rat could sense but not see the danger. *It's almost as big as I am,* Anton thought. *How am I going to do this?* But then his shoulders lowered and his head pulled in and a listening stillness ran along his spine from his head to his tail. He could see into the darkness, and his eyes focused upon the rat until there was nothing else in the world but Anton, crouched, and the doomed rodent below. The rat moved its head from side to side.

"I know you're there," it said, "and I'm ready for you." It took a step backward, then nervously looked over its shoulder. "Do you think I've never killed a cat before?"

Anton considered this. Was it possible? Or was this brute of a rat bluffing? Why not call its bluff. "Did you steal some poor kitten from its mother?" he said.

"Come on then," the rat said. "I'll kill you, too."

Anton sprang. Sensing the darkness closing over it, the rat rose up on its hind legs and bared its teeth. Anton caught the rat's snout in one set of claws, the meaty shoulder in the other, and dug in with all his strength. He swung his hindquarters

over the writhing back, sinking his back claws in just above the thrashing tail. The rat was strong and it struggled mightily, biting the air and shouting abuse.

"This ship's not big enough for the both of us!" it decreed.

"Have it your way," Anton said, and as he spoke, the rat wrested its head free and sunk its teeth into the soft pad of Anton's paw, which made him yowl and pull away. Thus freed, the rat twisted in its captor's grip.

"You're no match for me!" the rat cried. "You're dead!" With a sudden lurch, it latched on to Anton's throat.

Without fear or anger or so much as a thought, Anton grasped the rodent at the back of its neck and tore it loose from his throat. He had a good grip now.

"Not yet," he informed his opponent. Recapturing the rear end of the rat with his hind paws, Anton flattened the front end with a full set of claws in each shoulder. Then, opening his jaws wide and baring all his sharp teeth, he brought his mouth down at the base of the rat's skull and administered, with accuracy and speed, the killing bite. The sinewy body bucked once beneath him, the tail stood up straight then flopped to the floor. The rat was no more.

Anton bore down for another moment or two as his sense of who and where he was, and what he had just accomplished, filled his brain. Then he withdrew his claws and released his jaws, gagging at the fur and blood that came away in his mouth. He staggered as he stepped back, and the pain in his throat and paw reminded him this victory had come at a cost. He sat back on his haunches and examined the injured pad, going over and around it with his rough tongue. *Now what?* he thought. How was he to let the sailors know what he'd done?

The dead rat was still. Its shiny eyes had gone dull and flat; it was no longer a threat to anything. It was also, as far as Anton was concerned, not a fit meal either, and he was still groaningly hungry. The sailors were tucked in their cots, all but those on the deck for the night watch, and Cloudy wouldn't make his appearance in the galley until just before dawn. There would be no way to lure him in to see Anton's trophy; no, Anton would have to take the rat to the man and stick around long enough to make sure he got the connection—rat dead thanks to valiant effort of cat.

It was a loathsome business, and it took all Anton's energy to accomplish it. He took the rat's neck in his mouth again and lifted the creature like a kitten, though this smelly and heavy burden was as unlike a kitten as anything could be. Limping from his wounded paw, he carried it out along the hallway to the galley floor. When he had the rat inside the doorway, he dropped it and resolved to go no farther. A few more licks of the paw, and a bit of face cleaning, and then it was time to wait. He looked about the room, feeling hungry and tired. What a battle! If only Cecil were there, Anton would have such a story to tell, and Cecil would know just how fine a feat it was for a cat of Anton's sensitivity. *Good work, brother,* Cecil would say. Anton smiled at the next thought that crossed his mind, in Cecil's voice: *Put the rat on the table. It will say you care.*

It would be a struggle, but something made Anton certain it was the right thing to do. To present the rat in this way, to prove his good faith in doing his duty, should earn him the respect, and possibly the fish dinner, he knew he deserved.

Anton gazed upon the dead rat. He could get it up on the bench in one small leap, and then it might well be possible to fling himself and his prize onto the big cutting board. *Come along, mate,* Anton thought, as once again he took the rat's nape into his mouth. *We're going to make you look quite appetizing.*

Two skillful leaps and it was done. Anton arranged his offering, centered on the board with the tail straight out. Then, tired to his bones, he lay down on the far side of the table and fell instantly into a dreamless sleep.

He awoke to a shout. Cloudy was standing over him, his palms pressed against his cumulous beard, his eyes wide with alarm. "Lord, have mercy!" he said, taking in a long breath.

Anton sat up at once, trying to gauge the tone of this remark. Was it surprise, anger, outrage, gratitude? Cloudy gave his attention to the rat.

"Look at the dreadful beastie," he proclaimed. "He's of a size with ye. I hardly dare touch him for fear of contamination." He turned to the sideboard, took up a cloth and put it over the rat's middle, then picked up the corpse and headed for the deck. "Overboard with the devilish creature," he said.

Anton started to follow, but one step persuaded him he'd just as soon wait to see what happened next; his foot was sore, and he was weary, hungry, and still dazed from sleep. He heard voices above, Cloudy speaking to one of the sailors, then down the hatch appeared the shoes, legs, chest, and head of the cook, who stood for a moment, arms folded over his chest, gazing at Anton.

"But look at you, brave heart, the brute has wounded ye." He approached Anton mewing like a mother cat and brought his fingertips toward the fur on his neck. Anton's first thought was to run, but there was something in the manner of the man, a gentle concern that Anton had never experienced before, and so he steeled himself, as the fingertips came closer and closer, until, tenderly, the cook touched the bloody fur on his neck, drew his hand down Anton's side, and examined the deep cut on his paw. "You put up a fight, mate." Anton had to close his eyes, wondering what would happen next. If only it would be something to eat! As if the cook read Anton's thoughts, he turned away, pulled a tin pan from the sink rack, and went rummaging among the cans and bottles in the cupboard above his stove.

"No porridge for you this morning," Cloudy said. He took down a can, punctured it with a blade, poured out the thin white liquid into the tin, and set it before Anton on the table. "That's for starters," he said. Anton bent over the milk, sniffing carefully, then tested it with his tongue. It was good. He hunkered down to lap it up while Cloudy went back to his cupboard and took down another tin. This one he pried open with a different blade, and the aroma that issued from it made Anton sit up openmouthed, so that the milk ran down his chin. It was fish! Bite-size greasy fish such as Anton had never seen before, and Cloudy forked one, two, three into the pan. Their heads were crunchy; the little bones cracked against his palate delightfully—delicious, delicious, delicious. From deep in his chest Anton could feel the rumble of a purr running over his shoulders and down his back. He looked up at Cloudy, who held the tin in one hand, the fork in another, crooning to Anton. "That's to your taste, is it? I thought so, I thought so. Here, have another." When Anton was full, he sat down and slowly ran his tongue around his mouth, enjoying the last bits of the oil.

The hatch door was open and a soft breeze

passed through the galley, warm and damp as a summer's day on the harbor. Anton closed his eyes, feeling dreamy and gloriously full for the first time in days. Then he heard a sound that thrilled his heart, and he opened his eyes wide, turning his ears to locate the source. A singer with a voice high and sweet began a familiar melody. Anton stood up, strode to the end of the table, and leaped to the floor. His front paw stung him as he landed upon it, and he hobbled a few steps toward the door.

"So you like the shanties, do ye?" Cloudy said, following Anton to the few steps that led to the deck. Anton made his way up cautiously, and as he came out on the deck another singer joined in, and the song, to his great joy, was one of his favorites. *Windy weather boys, cloudy weather boys.* Anton had no idea what it meant, but the familiarity of it made him forget his fears, his wounds, his battle with the rat, the dark, hungry days in the storeroom— they all disappeared as he stepped out onto the deck to see the sailors gathered at the base of the enormous mainsail, which flapped softly in the warm, unsteady breeze. It was still dark, and the sky was black with a line of soft clouds drifting across the round face of the moon. Anton drew closer to the men and one of them noticed him, crouched there in the dark.

"There's Mr. Gray," Cloudy announced to his mates. "Our mighty little mate who slayed the blackguard stowaway. Let's give him a hand." To Anton's astonishment, the men paused in the song, all directing their gazes toward where he stood, and they began patting their hands together, just as they did at the saloon at the end of a show. Anton drew closer, all his senses alive. The sailors went back to their singing. Stars were fading above; the watery world around him seemed paused between night and day. He sat down near a coil of rope, feeling the change in his whiskers, breathing in the salty air, the sound of the voices in their forceful refrain. *When the wind blows, we're all together boys.*

Anton felt a shadow fall from above and looked up to see the moon. As he watched, the globe of light narrowed, shrouded in thick, dark clouds like folds of fur. It was like an eye, he realized, a great eye, the pupil long and narrow as a cat's eye, and it was watching him. A breeze rustled the hairs inside his ears, and it whispered to him as softly and clearly as Cecil did when he had a secret to tell. It whispered words Anton both did and didn't understand: "Where the eye sees the eye," the breeze said. Anton looked around, as if someone had spoken, but he was alone. The great ship surged beneath him, the sailors raised their voices, and Anton thought, *I'm a sailor now.* And this thought was curiously pleasant.

CHAPTER 8

A Fingerling Mist

A passing seagull, in the early morning hours, might have mistaken the once grand clipper where Cecil now found himself for a floating white three-ring circus tent missing its tallest center pole, sagging sadly in the middle. But there were no birds in sight, nor any other creatures interested enough to observe the poor ship, which had been dismasted in the storm the night before. With a terrifying crack the gale had snapped off the mainsail mast halfway down. The mast had landed on the starboard railing with a crash that had shaken Cecil awake and left him trembling. *We're sinking!* he thought miserably, and he resigned himself to the end, waiting grimly for the rising water to take the ship down in the night's complete darkness.

But the gray dawn revealed that they were not sinking after all, and now the crew and captain stood on the deck with their hands on their hips and their faces pinched into frowns, surveying the damage. Cecil crept out from his hiding place under the tarp and tried to take in what had happened.

The mainmast had clipped a spar of the aft mast on its way down and now lay with its topmost tip wedged in the rubble of the railing bars, the broken-off end still tangled in the rigging high above. Sails hung in drooping lengths like ragged laundry from the crossbars. Piles of rope and tarp lay in heaps on the deck, mixed with hunks of shredded wood and bits of seaweed.

The men looked up and down the fallen mast, inspecting it from every angle, shaking their heads. After a while a few of the younger crewmen retrieved boxes containing long curved needles and rolls of thick white thread, and set to work repairing the torn sails. Others slowly began setting things right on deck and clearing the debris. The captain, after much grumbling and cursing, finally pointed to the mast and shouted orders, where-upon the remaining ragtag collection of crewmen started cutting lines of rope off the mast and coil-ing it on the deck.

Over the next few days, Cecil sensed he was out of favor, distrusted and even reviled, and he stayed far away from the men and out of sight as much as he could. No one fed him, but luckily the storm's huge waves had tossed a fair quantity of fish onto the deck. Lodged in crevices between bales or behind posts, these were now largely ig-nored by the men. The sun smothered those on board from a cloudless sky, and there seemed to be no wind at all. Day and night passed, and passed again, as the repaired sails hung limply from their crossbars and the splintered mast lay on the deck. Scuffles broke out among the sailors, and their quick tempers made Cecil even more skit-tish. The men passed the time working on repairs, or swimming in the warm, flat water around the ship, and endlessly scanning the sky and horizon for some event, though both remained relentlessly empty.

❧ ❧ ❧

On the fourth day, gray clouds hung low, touching the ocean at the horizon, and a light rain fell steadily. The crew had retreated belowdecks, but Cecil remained above in the drizzle, tucked under a tent of ripped sailcloth. *Some fresh water, at least,* he thought as he watched the puddles slowly form. Ignoring his rumbling belly, he closed his eyes to nap, but his ears began to pick up another sound over the soft plinking of the rain on the deck, an irregular flapping coming from somewhere above. He peeked out and squinted upward. Wheeling toward the ship was a large dark gray bird, veering from side to side, its wings beating only intermittently. Cecil ducked back under the sail as the bird extended long red legs with black webbed feet to attempt a landing, but instead crashed into the mainsail mast and fell in a heap on the ratlines.

The sole crewman on deck lifted the brim of his hat, glared at the bird, then lowered the hat and went back to sleep. Cecil ventured another look around the edge of the sail. The bird had extracted itself from the ropes and flapped over to perch on the railing, where it fully extended its wings to either side and held them open, sitting very still and looking around. Cecil took careful note of the bird's long, hooked beak and sharp claws. Caution was in order. Birds were unintelligent and unreliable, in Cecil's view, but it had been days since he'd talked to any other creature, and he was desperate for company. He slowly advanced until the bird took notice of him.

"Say there, cat," said the bird, amiably enough. "How do?" Its face was bright orange, wrinkled and featherless except for two short tufts of white feathers that stood straight up above its eyes like fluttering white eyebrows, swaying lightly as it talked.

"I'm fine," said Cecil, though this was far from true. "I'm Cecil. You okay?"

"You can call me Shag," said the bird. "I'm all right. Trying to dry my wings here, heavy as rocks, and this rain isn't helping much." The little white feathers rippled as he shook his head in disgust.

Cecil kept his back legs tensed, ready to spring away if necessary. He'd never seen a bird this big before.

"Where are you headed?" Cecil asked, trying to sound casual.

Shag made a clucking sound in his throat. "The darnedest luck. Looking for some supper, saw a big bunch of bluefish moving fast, followed them for a while and lost my bearings in the clouds." He glared up at the sky. "Strength almost gave out, had to land on a crusty old whale, if you can believe that."

Cecil said nothing. *I can,* he thought.

"My island's still a ways off." Shag flicked his beak in the direction of the starboard bow. "But I spied this ship just sitting here . . ." He stopped and seemed to notice the way Cecil was keeping his distance. "Say, I'm a cormorant, you know. We don't eat things with legs, if that's what's worrying you." He cocked his head. "You're a cat who doesn't know his avian classification?"

"As far as I'm concerned," said Cecil, "there are two types of birds: the ones I can eat and the ones who can eat me. Does a seagoing bird like you know much about cats? Have you seen a small gray cat lately?"

The rain had stopped and the clouds thinned out to the west. "Nope, not lately," said Shag, rebalancing himself on the railing and turning to face the weak sun. "But I've seen plenty of cats. When you come across cats on ships, you've got three categories. The first is pets and they're pretty happy with their lot. Second, you've got your captives and they're all miserable. And third are the questers, looking for some sort of adventure, or else they're on a mission." He surveyed Cecil with round eyes of brilliant blue, like the harbor at Lunenburg on a sunny day. "So which kind are you?"

Cecil swallowed and looked away. "Questing, I'd say."

Shag nodded, then lowered his wings and glanced around the deck, which was strewn with pieces of mast and rigging.

"You got a big problem here," he observed.

"They're just about done fixing the mast," Cecil said. "We'll be on our way in no time." He nodded sagely. Saying it made him feel more confident.

Shag examined one of his talons. "Not in my experience, you won't."

"Oh really?" Cecil asked dryly.

Shag gestured with his wing at the broken mast. "From what I've seen, a busted mast like that doesn't get fixed." They both regarded the beheaded mast. "And ships with no sails don't get anywhere." He pointed to the sleeping sailor. "No food, no water. Your sailors will be skeletons soon. I've seen that happen."

Cecil's ears twitched. *Skeletons?* He sat up straight and studied Shag, who continued.

"You want my advice, you best get off this ship and I mean pronto," Shag said, lowering his beak and looking fixedly back at Cecil.

Get off the ship? A spark of panic lit inside Cecil for the first time. He had been assuming they'd get going eventually, but what if they stayed stuck? He was a cat, surrounded by miles and miles of ocean. If the ship didn't move, he'd be a skeleton soon, too.

Shag extended his wings again and beat them a few times to test them out. "Good to go." He turned on the railing to face the sea. "Well, best of luck to you, Cecil."

"Hang on!" cried Cecil. "Can you . . . take me with you? Carry me, I mean?" It sounded crazy, even to Cecil, but he felt desperate.

Shag turned back and looked at Cecil's generous frame. "Don't think we'd get far, would we?" His eyebrows fluttered in the breeze as he gazed out to the horizon. "Somebody'll come along for you, I'm betting. Somebody smarter than a little old bird." He looked sidelong at Cecil again, then sighed. "Here, I can leave you something to eat, at least." He leaned his head forward and made a coughing sound in his throat, and out of his beak and onto the deck flopped two good-size fish.

Cecil was astounded—this strange bird had been talking all this time with a couple of fish in his craw. "Thanks," he said weakly.

"So long," said Shag. In one powerful motion he launched himself from the rail.

Cecil watched him go, trying not to think about what the bird had said. The ocean looked endless and he felt lonelier than ever. With the ship drifting like a cork in a water barrel, he could see no means of escape, so he had to put the idea out of his mind for now.

Besides, the fish, it turned out, were still quite fresh.

❧ ❧ ❧

Two days later, on a blazing hot morning, Cecil went belowdecks in search of a cooler resting spot, always mindful of staying quiet and out of sight. Food and water were running low, and even the mice had disappeared—he had spotted one actually jumping overboard yesterday, shrieking incoherently, an unsettling sight. The repairs on the mainmast were not yet complete, so the ship was still drifting aimlessly.

At the sound of men clomping toward him from just beyond a corner, Cecil pushed past a slightly open door to his left into a small candlelit room. The room contained only a bed, a small desk, and a large, decrepit-looking sea chest on the floor. In the hallway the boots stomped nearer, along with the sound of arguing voices. Cecil slipped under the bed, the only place to hide, just as a man entered the room alone. The man shut the door, stepped to the chest, and, groaning with effort, lowered himself to his knees in front of it. Cecil piled all of his bulk into the farthest dark corner, trying to stay absolutely silent. He could see large rings on the man's fingers and lace sleeves on his coat and knew it must be the captain.

An uncomfortable quiet settled in the little room as Cecil held his breath, concentrating on not being discovered. He could only hear the raspy breathing of the captain and the small clicks of his rings as he placed his hands on the top of the chest. Finally Cecil breathed out slowly and crept forward to get a closer look. The chest was dented and scuffed on its painted surface. On the front face hung a large metal contraption with a loop on top threaded through a bolt, but the captain ignored that entirely and focused on the raised and decorated top. Cecil saw him trace the outline of a painted yellow fish with his finger, then turn his thumb down onto the fish and push. There was a sharp click inside the chest, and the hinged lid popped up and creaked softly as the captain lifted it.

Cecil's head thumped on the underside of the bed as he stretched his neck to see better, but the captain didn't notice as he stuck his hand down into what looked like layers of silky cloth packed into the chest. Gently he pulled out a little red cloth bag and loosened the strings holding it closed. He poured a small object out of the bag into his hand and held it in front of his eyes. It was the size of an acorn but round like a ball, and even in the dim room Cecil could see it clearly because it glowed with a pale light. The captain stared at it with his mouth slightly open, a tiny white full moon between his fingers, and Cecil was transfixed as well.

In the next moment, voices rose to shouting in the corridor and the captain dropped the stone into the bag and down into the chest, shutting the lid with a thud. Cecil skittered backward to avoid being seen. The captain struggled to his feet and whipped the door open, bellowing at the crew in the hall and waving his arms in agitation. Cecil shot out from under the bed and scrambled to the doorway, where the captain's tall black boots blocked most of the way out. Cecil leaped from side to side as the captain stepped back and forth and shouted orders. Finally Cecil backed up, timed his jump, and lunged between the captain's legs. He raced down the hall and up to the deck without looking back, the startled captain cursing him as he ran, which, he thought grimly, probably made a bad situation even worse.

※ ※ ※

Early in the afternoon, Cecil sat just inside a tipped-over crate near the port rail and pondered the state of things. There was the mystery of the captain's hidden stone, whatever it was, which gave Cecil an uncomfortable feeling as he had found that humans often fought over small, shiny objects. And what of the whale, whom he had not seen since the night of the storm? It had not returned either to rescue him or to finish the job of drowning him, and he didn't know if it wished him well or ill. Cecil felt restless on this immobile ship in the middle of this endless ocean, and he'd never find Anton on a ship that didn't move.

As he sat in the crate sifting through his problems, Cecil noticed small wisps of steam begin to rise up through the air over the water, vanishing in the sunlight. *Is it so hot that now the sea is boiling?* wondered Cecil. He roused himself, standing and stretching his back legs one by one, then stepped to the railing. Indeed the water, which had been dead calm since the storm, was simmering with tiny bubbles under the surface. Cecil glanced around to see if the men had noticed, but most of them were below decks taking a midday meal, and they could not man the crow's nest since the mast came down.

The bubbling waves began to make a faint hissing sound, and the steaming wisps became more densely packed, making the air hazy and vaporous. *That's actually kind of pretty,* Cecil thought, *and quite a bit cooler too.* One of the sailors awoke from a doze and looked around quizzically, then lumbered over to the below-decks door and called something down. Cecil doubled back and hopped up onto the crate for a better view. The haze steadily thickened, washing out the horizon line and muting the sunlight, and started to swirl, dancing in currents around the ship. Emerging from below decks, the captain and crew stood and stared. The haze condensed around the ship until it felt as if they were floating inside a cloud.

Abruptly, the younger sailors burst into laughter and slapped one another on the back. They waved their hands in the moist air and ran their fingers through their hair. Giggling, some romped about and held their mouths open as if to drink the air in, and Cecil noticed that he could not even see to the far end of the deck now through the thick haze. He watched the playful sailors, but he also saw the faces of the older crew, which were guarded and, Cecil thought, fearful.

Then an even stranger thing happened. The swirling mist developed long, thin tendrils that slipped through the air and began to wrap themselves around the arms and legs of the men, who pulled up short from their cavorting and glanced around nervously. Some of the men began backing away from the railings, watching the eddies with distrust, picking up their boots and trying to step gingerly out of the clouds. But the mist continued to thicken, and Cecil thought his eyes were playing tricks, for he imagined that he saw figures forming in the densest parts of the haze. The crew seemed to be having the same sorts of visions, whimpering softly and pointing at the empty air.

"What's this, then?" asked an older sailor, his voice high and thin. "Somebody there?"

Another swatted at the mist that drifted around his neck like a scarf. "*Somebodies,* more like," he grumbled, turning round and round.

"Can't be," snorted one of the younger fellows. "Just fog, mates." All the same he edged away from the fingers of murk reaching around his belly.

Cecil crouched low on the crate as he observed the heightening tension among the men. Foggy swirls had infiltrated every part of the deck and there was no getting away from them now. The white air was clammy and teased Cecil's nose and ears. He began to feel light-headed and thought he'd better move around a bit, but when he looked at the deck next to his crate he stopped short. There in the mist was a shape that very much resembled a large loaf of bread. His mouth watered at the thought. *Well! Wouldn't that be nice?* But as he gazed at it, the loaf grew legs and changed into the figure of a cat. A cat! *That would be less nice, though less lonely,* thought Cecil.

The mist cat was completely colorless. It stretched up with its front paws along the crate toward Cecil. He leaned over the top, trying to prepare an adequate greeting for something he wasn't sure was really there, when the cat suddenly extended its misty claws and hissed violently at Cecil.

"Oh, is that how it is?" Cecil said out loud, his voice surprisingly muted in the haze. He flattened his ears, bared his teeth, and took a long, hard swipe down the side of the crate with his paw, only to feel it pass right through the cat figure's head with a wet breeze. He pulled back and the cat slid up to the top of the crate in a sinewy motion and sat hunched, eye to cloudy eye with Cecil.

"Okay," Cecil said, assessing the situation. "Crate's all yours!" he called out, and bounded off the other side.

Plunging through the fog on deck, Cecil scampered through the door that led to the officers' quarters. The air was clear down below, and as Cecil strolled aimlessly about he noticed that the door to the captain's room stood ajar. He slipped in and leaped atop the chest. The whole surface was carved with pictures of fish, an entire school of them, and he was momentarily flustered. Which

ANTON AND CECIL ~ *113*

one was it? It was up in the corner, yes, but was it red or green or . . . ? Cecil could hear the crew crashing above, and he began frantically stepping on the fish with his paws, trying to push down just the way the captain had done. Press, press, press . . . *was it the yellow one?* Press, *click!* The chest popped open and flipped Cecil back onto the floor on his head. He quickly recovered to his feet, dashed around to the front, and pushed his nose through the opening. Snatching the little red bag with his teeth, he turned and bolted back up the stairs, a black streak with a prized possession.

On deck, the mist still swirled about the sailors, wrapping them in its tendrils and whispering in their ears. The crazed crew ran around batting the misty swirls, picking up hooks, hammers, and buoys from the deck and throwing them at the haze, knocking about other crewmen in the turmoil. Cecil quickly hid his treasure in a coil of rope near the mainsail mast. Ducking the flying objects and staggering crewmen, he looked for the captain and found the poor man rooted to one spot, struggling for control of both himself and his crew.

Holding his arms tightly around his chest, the captain jumped up onto a barrel and shouted, "'Tis but a fingerling mist I tell you! Stand still, men, or it will drive ye mad!'"

This advice did little to comfort the distraught sailors. Two old fellows had straddled the ship's rail, as if to throw themselves into the sea to escape the invisible horrors, when the entire scene silently began to reverse course. The figures slowly faded from Cecil's view, the fingers of mist retreating back into the surrounding cloud. The men regained their footing and lurched together in a clump on the deck, clutching each other and glancing up and down warily. All was still, the haze settling in a ring over the waves surrounding the ship.

In the quiet, Cecil had an odd, prickly sensation in his whiskers. Something cast a faint glow of light over the spot where he stood, and he looked up. The foggy cloud was still thick over the tops of the masts, but directly above him Cecil saw a brighter patch forming, oblong, with a darker swath in the center. *Must be the sun,* he thought, *burning through the mist.* The pale light brightened further and he felt warmed by it, held in it somehow. A long moment passed, and then the light faded rapidly. Cecil felt chilled in its absence, and a little lonely. He looked back at the crew, but none of them were looking up where the light had been. *Strange,* he thought.

Over the hissing of the haze came another sound of heavy, churning water. Cecil pressed himself against the mast and pricked up his ears. *Now what?* he wondered, trying to disguise his substantial girth as a bundle of sailcloth. The fog off the bow of the ship was changing, thinning and darkening. Turning toward this new unknown, the men as a group took a step back in hushed fear. The wall of mist continued to dissolve bit by bit, and the churning grew louder and more powerful, until at last the mist dropped away entirely to reveal an astounding sight.

Looming above them, only yards away, was a vast brigantine under full sail.

Cecil's knees collapsed under him and the crew gasped in one giant intake. Blood-red flags flew on every mast, and leaning against the brig's railing was a cohort of grinning buccaneers. They were remarkably ugly, with missing teeth and gashed faces. Cecil might have laughed at their comical enthusiasm as they strained to get close enough to jump the gap and board the clipper, were it not for the impressive object each pirate held menacingly above his head—a long and glinting sword.

The cormorant's words flashed in Cecil's mind: "Get off the ship." *And here's an opportunity!* Suddenly energized, Cecil quickly surveyed the brigantine. She looked strong and trim, with all her rigging intact, unlike his own ship. The leering crew was well-fed, judging from the size of their overhanging bellies, and Cecil caught the scent of smoked meats wafting over on the breeze. *A pirate's life for me is what I always say, no?* Cecil ducked out of sight and waited for his chance. The pirate crew now began climbing the ratlines up the mast poles to the overhanging spars, where long ropes were fastened and coiled. With wild abandon and whooping war cries, they gripped the rope ends, leaped off the spars, and swung in long semicircles over to Cecil's ship, landing more or less on their feet with swords brandished. *They've done this before,* thought Cecil with admiration.

This new development shocked the clipper crew out of their stupor, and having no swords themselves, they grabbed whatever was at hand to mount a defense. Working efficiently, the pirates overwhelmed and pinned the sailors to the deck, quickly searching their pockets for anything of value. Cecil saw a swordsman neatly slice away a leather pouch of coins stashed inside the shirt of a passing sailor and held around his neck by a cordon, leaving the sailor lying dazed and gasping for breath. *No time like the present,* thought Cecil, and headed for the ratlines, stopping briefly by the coil of rope to retrieve the small red bag hidden there.

The ropes leading up were tied in a lattice pattern to form a kind of ladder stretching from the deck up to the spars that held the sails above. Cecil balanced along the lines, trying to move speedily but carefully, clambering up to the nearest long spar and then out to its farthest tip in the direction of the pirate ship. *Too far to jump,* he figured, and looked around hurriedly for another way. The captain emerged from the below-decks doorway, cursing with rage, his black eyes finding Cecil, the red pouch dangling from his mouth, up on the spar.

"Blast you, you thieving blackguard!" he roared. "Give me back my pearl!" The captain began shoving crewmen out of his way, advancing toward the lines. A seemingly endless stream of pirates

continued to swing across the breach between the ships.

Here we go! Cecil thought merrily as a howling pirate soared through the air toward him. The pirate let go and landed on the deck, and as the rope swung on past, Cecil held his breath and jumped. He dug all four sets of claws into the rope and clung fiercely as he swung back toward the pirate ship, still holding the red bag between his clenched teeth. The sickening drop carried him over his own deck, past the ocean between the two ships, and up over the deck of the brigantine.

Dropping in! What's for supper? He sheathed all his claws quickly. Sliding partway down the rope and free-falling through the air, Cecil crash-landed awkwardly on top of the captain's map room, then rolled off the roof and down to the deck with a thud. *Ooof!* He opened his eyes and looked for a place to hide the red bag, though his head was reeling from the fall. A knothole in one of the deck boards behind a post would have to do for a hiding spot. He pushed the bag down into the hole with his nose, then looked around to get his bearings.

As Cecil began walking unsteadily across the deck, he heard a soft voice, barely a whisper, coming from a nearby doorway: "Hey! In here." Cecil stumbled over to the door and slipped inside. In the dim light of the room he peered at the owner of the voice, hoping it wasn't another strange, insubstantial figure, and it was not. It was a small white cat, a real one, with a band of black fur across her eyes.

"Gretchen?" Cecil asked, astonished.

CHAPTER 9

Marooned

Anton missed his brother and he missed his home, but it was in his nature to make the best of what he had, and he found much of interest in his new life. For days fair weather and light breezes spurred the *Mary Anne* upon her way. The air was fresh and the sailors in good humor. Anton found the deck a pleasant place for an evening stroll, and when the sailors gathered at the base of the mainmast and the accordion player ran through the scales on his instrument, the small gray cat was always nearby. One afternoon, as he stepped out from the galley door, he saw a marvelous sight—winged silver fish flying over the deck. One, two, three ran afoul of the masts or the sails and flopped onto the deck where the sailors caught them with glee. That night, at dinner, Anton found two tasty heads in his dish.

What amazed him was the expanse of sea that stretched out forever in every direction. He looked out from the prow, from the stern, from atop the cabin, nothing but sea, sea, sea. On some days it was deep blue with little whitecaps. On others it was sparkling with light. One morning he noticed the sailors scampering up the masts and gathering in the sails. He climbed up on the bridge and looked out at the churning water. The sky was dark and the water was the color of lead. Then he felt the first drops of the coming downpour. Cloudy stood in the open doorway, looking up at the sky with a deep frown. Anton hustled past him to his favorite napping place under the sink.

And there Anton stayed while the ship was tossed about like a bauble, rain poured in through the hatches, the wind roared so fiercely the sailors could hardly hear each other, and no food stayed in a pan. No one, including Anton, got anything to eat but hard bread and tinned meat for two days.

Then, as suddenly as it had come, the storm ceased, the sky turned bright blue, and the clouds disappeared. The sailors climbed the masts and dropped down great sheets of sail, which were filled out by a fair breeze. Anton came out of the galley and climbed atop the cabin, where he saw a beautiful sight. Dead ahead was the pale outline of an island with trees at the shoreline and mists at the high peaks. It was small, but it was growing larger every minute. A wide beach came into view, a place no doubt rich with crabs. Anton watched attentively as the captain yelled orders and the sailors shifted the booms. The island was their destination.

There was no harbor, so they lowered anchor offshore and commenced dropping small boats into the shallows. The sailors were going ashore and leaving Anton behind. He wanted to run on that beach. As the last boat was being lowered from the side, Anton caught the rope between his front paws and swung down until he was close enough to let go and land in Black Top's lap. A cheerful shout went up among the sailors, and Anton was passed from hand to hand until he was wedged into a seat at the stern, safe from the surging movement of the oars. When the boat's prow rammed into the sand, the sailors clambered out and pulled it onto the shore. Anton leaped out.

He had never really been on a beach. There was a little sand among the big rocks near the lighthouse at home and another bit at the end of the wharf, but this was a meadow of sand. It was surprisingly hot, and his paws sunk into it. He couldn't get any traction, but after a few tries he discovered he could leap by pushing off hard from both back paws. There was a grove of odd trees with bark like shingles and fronds like enormous dark green spiders about fifty leaps away, and Anton set off in their direction. The sailors wading in from the shallows shouted to him, "Mr. Gray, Mr. Gray," but he paid no heed. It took all his energy and concentration to make his leaping progress out of that miserable sand.

At last he arrived in the pleasant grove. The soil was sandy but hard, and a soft breeze rustled the trees. Anton walked around a tree, enjoying ground that didn't shift under his paws. How wonderful to be on land. He sat down on a smooth rock that seemed designed for a cat's comfort, and, slowly turning his head, he took in the scene. There was a thin stream running toward the sea in easy reach, lined by tall grasses that nearly hid it from view. In those grasses, Anton thought, he would find something crunchy, and in the stream perhaps little minnows to scoop up and swallow whole. So this was where the great ships went, and no wonder. It was warm, and there was water and fresh, delicious food. If you stayed off the beach, it was paradise.

Suddenly, Anton heard a noise that made his fur stand on end. It came from above, a screech such as a mouse might emit on capture, but a thousand times as loud. Anton sat up and followed the sound with his eyes. There, awkwardly balanced on one of the tree fronds, was the biggest and strangest bird he'd ever seen. Its neck was long, like a dull gray snake. Its plumage was black. Its head looked like it was made of pink rubber, with swollen raisins for eyes and a brown beak thick as a horse's hoof and curved to a sharp point. Its claws were as big as Anton's paws. It was a monster of a bird. As Anton watched, it opened and closed its pincerlike beak. It let out another screech. "Dinner is served," it croaked. Then it dived right at Anton.

Maybe not paradise.

Anton made a dash for the grass as the bird

strafed him from above. It let out another scream in pursuit, but couldn't pull itself out of the dive and crashed into a bramble bush, croaking and thrashing hysterically. *What a poorly designed bird,* Anton thought as he crept toward the water, keeping his head down. His instinct proved a sound one, for there were flat rocks in the burbling water of the stream, which made it easy to scamper to the other side, where a grove of real trees with limbs promised both shade and shelter. The bird had evidently given up for now.

Anton stopped and had a long drink of the cool water, then sauntered into the trees. In the distance he could hear the sailors calling to one another on the shore, busy with some collecting enterprise. There was a comfortable seat of mossy roots at the base of a tree, and he settled there thinking a nap might be in order before heading back to the beach. Almost at once sleep came over him. He dreamed he was with Sonya and Cecil, curled up by the lighthouse while the water lapped at the rocks. Then there was rustling nearby, something drawing close to them in the dark, and he thought it was a rat.

Anton opened his eyes as a shudder ran up his spine. There *was* a rustling sound, and it was coming from all around him. He sat up and slowly turned his head from one side to the other. He was surrounded by the huge, ungainly birds. They were closing in on him, clacking their beaks and rustling their wings as they approached.

"Hungry, hungry, hungry," they chanted in their eerie, humanlike voices. Without a thought, Anton took the nearest exit—straight up the tree. The birds paced around the trunk, gazing up at him and screeching. One, then another, tried to fly up, but they were awkward and clumsy, like turkeys. Anton had wedged himself in the crook of a limb where they couldn't quite get at him. One made it to the end of the limb and sat there eyeing him, but not moving. "Oh hungry," he said. "Dinner, dinner." Anton swatted the bird with all his strength and every claw out, and the bird, dodging the blow, lost his grip and tumbled down the tree to join his friends below. He could keep them at bay, one by one, Anton thought, but how was he going to get down from the tree?

Hours passed. The ugly birds had staked him out at the bottom of the tree and they seemed indifferent to time. Sometimes a few new ones arrived and a few went away. At one point three of them flew up over the tree and circled in the air lazily. Anton couldn't see the beach from his perch, but he could hear the sailors moving about, shouting to one another. As the sun began to set, he heard a sound that frightened him; it was Cloudy, walking along the shore calling, "Mr. Gray, Mr. Gray."

Anton cried out, "Here, I'm here," but the breeze was against him and carried his voice away. Shadows began to creep across the floor of the woods, and the birds grew quiet. Anton stayed in his treetop perch, battling sleep all through the long night. He could hear them moving about, cackling at one another. They had one subject: hunger. Toward dawn the world grew quiet, and the only sound was the distant water combing and combing the shore. At last a pale green light flushed up from the forest floor, and Anton looked down to see that the birds were gone.

He was down the tree in a moment and on the run to the beach. He bounded through the marsh grass at the edge of the stream, thinking about nothing but getting back on the boat. But when he came at last to the water's edge, he saw that not only the small boat but the *Mary Anne* herself was gone. He was marooned.

All that day and the next Anton fended for himself, ever on the alert for the birds. He hid in the grasses by the stream and caught various tiny fish and shellfish, which were actually tasty, and the water was fresh, so he had plenty to drink. At night he crouched under a large piece of driftwood near the beach. It was damp and very cold, but he was safe there—the birds didn't like the beach any better than he did—so there he stayed. On the third day he found a picked-over skeleton of some animal near the stream. It looked like a very large gopher, with a flat leathery tail—the only piece the monster birds hadn't stripped away from the bones.

Anton went back to his driftwood lair. Just before dark he came out again. As he was poking about in the shallows of the stream, he glanced up to see a circlet of black feathers, rising above a mass of fern at the edge of the forest. The monster birds.

Anton froze, one paw in the air, his head lowered, bringing his haunches down low so that he could bolt in any direction. He turned his ears forward and listened with all his attention, but the sound he heard didn't make sense. It wasn't a noise the birds made, but rather a faint *th-th-th-th-th* and then *grmmp,* like water running down a clogged drain. The feathers rustled in the faint breeze, moved forward, then stopped. "*Th-th-th-th-th-th. Grmmp.*" Anton was perfectly motionless, in a state of pure alertness that could outlast anything alive. "*Th-th-th-th-th. Grmmp.* Ugh." The ferns parted, and the strangest animal he'd ever seen stepped out into the open.

Anton did recall a much smaller, featherless version of this creature. When he and Cecil were kittens, Cecil had caught and eaten a few as they dashed among the stones at the base of the lighthouse, but even Cecil found them indigestible. Lizards they were called, but those were skittery brownish things, no longer than a claw, with tiny heads and detachable tails. This one was as big as a dog. Its skin was wrinkly and greenish blue. The protruding black eyes operated independently, the mouth stretched halfway round the oblong head, and the tongue was a blood-red whip, which flicked out distractedly. It was the flicking tongue that made the *th-th-th* sound. Strangest of all, the creature's cheeks, neck, and shoulders were studded with black feathers. The lizard took another step, one eye coming to rest on Anton while the

other focused on its own fearsomely clawed front foot. "Good grief. What are you?" the lizard said. "Some kind of weasel?"

Anton put his paw down and lifted his head. "I'm a cat," he said.

The lizard opened its mouth, showing the red roof of its palate, then closed it again and flicked the tongue out and in. "Never heard of that," it said.

"I was on a ship and I got stranded here."

"That explains it. No telling what comes off those things. A creature that called himself a weasel got left here once. He had fur like you. He didn't last long."

"He died?"

"He did. And then the clackers got him." The lizard's eyes spun up and around, scanning the sky and the brush. "What's your name?" it asked.

"Anton."

"I'm Dave," said the lizard.

"Why do you have feathers? Are you part—what do you call them?"

"I don't know their real name," Dave admitted. "I just call them the clackers because they never shut up." He opened and closed his mouth again.

Anton couldn't tell if it was purposeful or just a tic. "And no, I'm no bird," Dave concluded. "It's just that I like to eat clacker eggs. They're really good. Have you tried them?"

"I've just been trying not to wind up like the weasel."

"Right. Well, I'm a lot bigger than you. And the truth is the stupid clackers make a lot of threats, but they never kill anything. They just chase you and circle around you and try to scare you to death, and then they pick your bones. That's what they did to the weasel. I don't pay any attention to them; I just want the eggs, so they get all excited and I have to fight them off, and their feathers are really sticky. If I get a few in my mouth it takes all day to pull them out, and it hurts."

"But the eggs are worth it."

"Well, there's not a lot of variety on this island."

Anton considered this. "And if you eat the eggs, there are fewer clackers."

"Right. Say, you've got nice-looking little paws. Have you got good claws in those?"

Anton raised his forepaw and popped out his claws.

"Wow," said Dave. "Retractable."

"Useful," Anton agreed.

"Do you think you could pull some of these feathers off my shoulders? I can't reach them, they stick me when I move, and I'm really sick of looking like a bird."

Cautiously, Anton approached the lizard and stood looking up at the feathers, which hung at odd angles from the leathery hide. "Put your head down so I can reach them," he said, and Dave obeyed, dropping down on his haunches and resting his lower jaw on the ground. Anton eased a paw around a big feather and pulled it as best he could, but his pads slipped off. He tried again, pinching the feather between his claw and pad. With a tug it came loose.

"Great," Dave said. "Do a few more."

Anton pulled feathers from Dave's shoulders while Dave asked him questions. "So," he said. "You come from the land of cats."

"Well," Anton replied. "Not just cats. But there are a lot of us."

"And you all know each other."

"I don't know all cats, but I know all the ones who live on the docks. Do you know the other lizards here?"

"There aren't many of us, so I pretty much know everyone. But we don't spend time together."

"Don't you get lonely?"

"Not really. We're cold-blooded, you know."

"Oh," said Anton, though he didn't quite understand.

"Are you lonely? Do you miss other cats?"

"I miss my brother. Do you have a brother?"

"Not so you could call it that. We come from eggs."

"Oh, I'm sorry," said Anton, confused. "I had no idea."

"It's okay. It's natural. So what's your brother like?"

"He's a lot bigger than me, he's mostly black, and he's very brave, but he's foolhardy. There, now you don't look like a bird."

Dave got to his feet and stood, turning his head from side to side. "That's great," he said. His eyes rolled about on their separate quests, and he opened and closed his mouth again. "Will you look at that sky," he said. "Something weird is going on." Anton followed Dave's roving left eye. The sun had set, the sky had darkened, and a thick blanket of pale clouds unrolled toward the land from the horizon. As Anton and one of Dave's eyes watched, the clouds parted overhead, and a bright stream of moonlight, like a moving white finger, pointed at the beach just beyond where he and the lizard stood. Then Anton saw the spooky phenomenon he had glimpsed once before: an eye, a cat's eye, gazing down at him from the clouds.

Dave studied the heavenly cat's eye with one of his eyes and the real cat with the other. "To me, that eye looks a lot like your eye."

"Do you think?" said Anton.

"You know what they say about the eye," said Dave.

"No," said Anton, though he did remember *some*thing. "What do they say?"

The lizard sat back on his haunches and managed to get both eyes focused straight ahead, reciting in a deep, sonorous voice, "Where the eye sees the eye, the lost shall be found."

"And who are they?"

Dave relaxed, doing his open-and-close-mouth routine. "Who are who?"

"The ones who say that?"

"That's a really good question. I never thought about it, because I never lost anything."

"Right," said Anton. Lizard and cat gazed seaward, following the bright beam as it moved beyond the beach and over the water.

"Holy chameleon," Dave said. "Do you see what I see?"

Anton did see, but he could hardly believe his eyes. He closed them tight, then opened them again. It was a beautiful silvery ship, outlined in white like a drawing on dark paper, anchored before the horizon, its sails furled and its flag fluttering in the thin shore breeze.

A ship! Anton let out a cry.

"That must be your ride," Dave said.

Anton frowned, gazing out at the ship. It had only two masts, so it wasn't the *Mary Anne*. Dave might be right—it could be a way off the island, but how was he going to get to it?

"This is big," Dave continued, gazing up again. "I've never seen anything like this before."

Anton nodded, looking up as well, but the streaming finger of light had disappeared, and the cat's eye was gone. Then, as they looked back to the shore, a more amazing sight met their eyes. Three black rocks rose up in the shallows, like magical stepping-stones. A breeze, or was it a shiver, seemed to draw Anton along and he stepped out onto the sand. At once from the forest, he heard a less mysterious sound, the screams of the clackers gathering into a vicious cloud. They had spotted him.

Dave started talking fast, his eyes moving around in opposite directions, taking in everything, the ship, the stones, the clackers. "Okay," he said. "I think I get it. You don't have much time. Make a run for those rocks and don't look back. The clackers will chase you but they can't land in the sand—they fall over—and they won't go far from shore, so you should be able to make it, but you need to go fast and you need to go now."

The enormous birds were rising over the treetops. "Dinner," screamed one.

Another shrieked, "Dead meat."

"You're right," Anton said. "Wish me luck."

"Good luck," said Dave. "Nice to meet you. Give my regards to the land of cats."

"Thanks," Anton said. "I will." And then he sprinted for the water, not looking back. He could hear the rush of wings behind him and the screaming avian mob descending from above. One dived and crashed in front of Anton, falling on its side in the sand, its claws battling the air. Anton tore past the sputtering bird. Another tried for an eaglelike swoop from behind and caught Anton's tail in its talons. Anton yelped and turned on the bird, digging his claws into one of the wings, which served to make the clacker open its beak, but still the bird held on with its talons. Anton sunk his teeth into the wing, pulling away with a mouthful of feathers. Then he leaped forward, nearing the water's edge. The clacker took a bit of cat flesh as it bounced off, stumbling in the sand like a drunken sailor.

At last Anton was at the shoreline and leaping for the first rock. He landed, gripping with his claws, expecting a slippery surface that would give him no purchase, but to his surprise the rock had a leathery quality that allowed him to pull himself easily upon it. He sprang from the first rock to the second, and then to the third, which was wider and well above the water. The clackers had pulled up, a mass of shrieking feathers, but the higher they went, the more graceful they became, until in a loose, swirling squadron, they circled overhead and turned back toward their island.

That was when Anton felt the rock shift beneath his paws. It was rising, shedding water from all sides. The smaller pieces behind him sank, disappearing in the shallows. The rock was moving out away from the shore, slowly at first, but then picking up speed. Anton dug in all his claws and stared into the darkness. Ahead he could make out the ship, its running lanterns glittering and reflected in the water like a double line of fallen stars. More and more of the leathery rock was exposed until a round black hole, spewing seawater like a fountain, broke through the surface of the water. "Great cats in heaven," Anton whispered. "I'm on a whale."

And then it was full whale speed ahead, so fast that Anton's fur was flattened in the draft and the salt spray flew up and stung his eyes. The ship grew bigger and bigger, until he could see two sailors on the deck, and another descending from the rigging. A tremor ran along his arched spine—were they going to ram into the ship? The whale slowed and Anton had a moment to take in the ship, rocking softly in the calm sea, the anchor line taut off the stern. The whale veered sharply toward that rope, bringing his passenger within an easy leap, then gradually submerging until Anton really had no choice but to jump. He scrambled up the rope and threw himself over the stern with an *umph* of relief. What a ride!

Unbeknownst to Anton, he wore across his shoulders an honorary mantle of black feathers. He stood on his hind legs, his front paws pressed to the rail, and looked down to see his silent rescuer. In the swinging light over the stern he could just make out the enormous creature, rolling smoothly onto his side so that his great barnacled eye came into view. Anton, with a shiver, saw that the immense beast was looking up at the very small, wet, grateful cat.

He heard the shouts of the approaching sailors, who had at last spotted the whale. "Thank you, thank you, Mr. Whale," Anton called, as his rescuer dived back to his watery home below the surface and sped away.

CHAPTER 10

Gretchen's Tale

As the pirate raid of the clipper ship carried on raucously outside the small room, Gretchen and Cecil faced each other in astonishment.

"I can't believe it!" Cecil purred, swishing his tail back and forth. "Aren't you Gretchen from back home? It's me, Cecil! You remember me from around the docks, right?" Cecil bobbed his head as the white cat stared at him with wide gray eyes. She said not a word. Had she forgotten her home village already?

"You were taken, weren't you?" Cecil asked in

a lower voice. "That's what we heard. Awful story!" He looked closely into her face. Was she embarrassed? Did she not remember him at all? "My brother, Anton, was impressed, too, right off the dock in broad daylight if you can believe it." Cecil waited for her to speak.

"I'm Gretchen," she said finally, her voice low and cold. She paused, looking away. "But no one calls me that here."

Cecil leaned back, casting his eyes around in the dim light. "Here, eh?" He chuckled. "So where *is* here?" he asked. "What happened to you?"

"Long story," she said shortly. She turned back to Cecil and sighed. "I never expected to see anyone from back there again."

"Back there? *Home,* you mean?" Cecil asked, surprised. "Well, I don't know about you but *I'm* sure glad to see a familiar face."

"I just never expected it," Gretchen repeated. She paused and looked toward the door. "I could show you around the ship. Are you hungry?"

Cecil nodded. "My favorite question." He thought about showing her the stone he had hidden, but her manner made him hesitate. She was strange, distant in a way. She didn't seem happy to see him.

"Come on then," Gretchen said. They walked to the doorway and stepped out into the late afternoon haze.

※ ※ ※

The starboard side of the vessel was away from the mayhem of the raid, and the two cats sniffed through boxes on the deck in search of food. Cecil hadn't eaten well for quite some time, and smells of spices, cheeses, and tangy meats were all around. After they found a suitable cache of cheese and fish to snack on, Gretchen began to tell her story.

"Getting impressed in the first place was really stupid. I never thought it would happen to me," she said briskly. "I always liked fishing at night."

Cecil swallowed a chunk of fish. "Didn't Billy ever tell you—"

"About the danger?" Gretchen snorted. "Of course. Everyone told me, but I thought I was too smart to be captured, too quick anyway." She looked up, as if remembering. "But there I was, stuck in a dark hold, my head pounding, and the next time I saw daylight the ship was surrounded by water. That was it." She shook her head bitterly.

Cecil noticed a long scar running across her

neck and shoulder. "Rough times, were they?" he asked.

She picked at a slab of cheese and shrugged. "On that ship, the crew were mean and mad all the time. The captain spent most of the days sleeping and the men were always fighting each other. They thought to kick me if they saw me, but nobody thought to feed me. It was almost a relief when the buccaneers attacked us and took me along with the loot. That's how I got to be here. *Much* more interesting." Cecil saw a glint of amusement in her eyes. She looked up at him quickly, returning to the present. "Were you taken, too, then?" she asked.

"No," replied Cecil, and the weight of his mission slid back over him like an anvil. "I have to find Anton, so I stowed away to follow him. Though, actually, I don't know if I'm following, or just lost . . . It's bigger out here than I imagined." He gestured widely with his paw.

Gretchen's mouth dropped open. "You're telling me you got on a ship voluntarily, and you're searching the whole ocean for your brother?" she asked, her voice rising. "That's . . . crazy."

"Yeah, tell me about it," said Cecil, leaning back

to gaze at the intricate rigging and billowing red flags high above their heads. "Kind of fun, though, I have to say."

"And brave," Gretchen added softly, dropping her eyes back to the cheese.

�֍ ✤ ✤

"What *is* all this stuff, anyway?" Cecil asked as they made their way through a maze of boxes and barrels, heading toward the stern of the ship. The men moved among the piles, stacking crates on top of other crates and dragging stuffed seabags to stand leaning against one another. Often they stopped their work to root through the contents, snarling or snorting depending on what they discovered of worth.

"This is all the stuff that we've taken on from other ships," explained Gretchen, sniffing curiously at the new cargo.

"*We*," Cecil repeated. "Interesting. You think of yourself as part of the crew, do you?"

Gretchen sent him a tepid look. "Some things you just get used to," she said, as she turned to walk ahead.

Eager to show off his shipboard savvy, Cecil crouched to spring up to a nearby barrelhead. "I

usually like the view from on top of one of these
to get my bearings."

"Wouldn't do that," she said, not looking back.

Cecil leaped, but the barrel was open and full
of rice. His paws sank down and he flailed for a
few seconds, sloshing grains onto the deck, until he finally scrambled out, shaking his fur from
head to tail. A pirate grabbed the handle of his
cutlass and swung it at Cecil, narrowly missing his
ears. Cecil dived between two barrels and caught
up with Gretchen.

"Whoa!" he exclaimed, his eyes wide. "That
was close."

Gretchen was unfazed. "It's no big deal," she
said coolly, leading them up to a ledge by the rail
where they could look out over the water. "That's
just the way they are."

Cecil watched her face. "So your life hasn't been
easier here," he said.

Gretchen surveyed him for a moment, as if considering what to say. "When I first came aboard,
there was already a cat here—a fat, lazy, ginger-
colored cat. I learned to do her job better than
she did. She didn't care for that and began attacking me while I slept." She stopped and licked

her shoulder a few times, where the long scar ran from her jawline. "It took a while, but I figured out how to defend myself—I fought the ginger cat and won—and afterward she was terrified of me and worthless to the crew. The captain finally dumped her onto a packet ship we raided. *That* was a good day." A smile of satisfaction briefly lit her hard face. She turned back to him. "So now it's my ship," she finished simply.

Cecil sat looking at her, wide-eyed. "Wow, that must have been tough." He cocked his head. "Nice scar, though," he said with a small smile. "It makes you look worldly, like you can take care of yourself. But you're too thin. You need to eat more."

Gretchen gave him a smirk. "Well, you look like you've been eating well enough. In fact, a diet might be a good idea." As Cecil surveyed his own bulk—he thought he'd lost weight—she resumed her role as tour guide, turning to the crew at their work. "The men here obey the captain, which makes life easier," she said. "I know how to stay on his good side. He gave me a name; Pearl, he calls me. They all do. Sometimes they laugh at me and hold their fingers around their eyes, making fun of my black mask, I guess, but none of them has the courage to hurt me."

Cecil was startled by a strange thought. "Have *you* seen your black mask?" he asked slowly.

Gretchen closed her eyes, as though considering something. When she opened them again, she said, "Follow me. I'll show you," and she hopped down from the ledge and moved off between the barrels without looking back.

Cecil sat for a moment longer, inhaling the briny ocean breeze. Gretchen was quite an adventurer, all right—a pirate cat through and through. The question was, did she want a friend, or did she want to be left alone? A gray-bearded crewman stomped toward Cecil and he decided it was time to move along.

❖ ❖ ❖

They had to pass through the port side of the ship, which was where the action was. They crouched under a box on its side to avoid getting hit by falling items, and watched the scene. The men were still swinging on the long ropes attached to the crossbars, sailing across to Cecil's old clipper with wild abandon, laughing loudly and singing snatches of bawdy songs. They seemed to be having a delightful time, although Cecil thought there really couldn't have been *that* much to plunder on the other ship.

Sometimes one of the pirates lost his grip on the rope and sprawled across one or the other decks, or dropped into the sea between the ships and had to be fished out by men with ropes hanging over the sides. Undaunted, smiling, the dunked sailor jumped back and shimmied up the ratlines again. If a crewman successfully swung back to the pirate ship and got his feet planted on the spars once more, he dropped whatever loot he had onto the deck before taking off again.

Cecil craned his neck to look up at the men on the crossbars. They seemed to be slowing down, taking fewer trips across. "Do they always swing over like this? Doesn't a lot of good stuff get broken this way?" he asked as a small chest crashed on the deck and burst open.

Gretchen chuckled softly. "They do love to swing, it's true. Let's have a look at what's coming in."

Gretchen carefully picked her way through the piles and the wreckage spread across the deck planks. Her eyes searched back and forth over the booty. Cecil followed, watching her keenly till he caught a whiff of roasted meat and turned aside to hunt for it. He spotted a large bone with a bit of meat still clinging to it. *Ham! I love ham,* he thought happily.

"Ah, here we go," said Gretchen quietly. Cecil turned back to see her grasping a thin piece of cord with her teeth and tensing her back legs to pull it out from underneath a heap of coats.

"What's special about string?" he asked, dropping his ham bone. Gretchen didn't answer, but continued to tug on the cord until it slid free from the pile. It was attached to a small canvas pouch, similar to the one Cecil had brought over. She laid the pouch flat on its side on the deck and, beginning at the bottom, began stepping quickly with her paws on the canvas, like she was dancing a little jig, working her way up to the top. At the cinched-up mouth of the pouch she pushed swiftly down with both paws, and out rolled a round blue stone of lustrous beauty.

Cecil caught only a glimpse of the stone, how it was carved with many tiny flat sides, how it reminded him of the dark sea at night lit with cool sparkles of moonlight, before Gretchen scooped it into her mouth and moved off at a fast trot.

"Be ri' b'k," she murmured, her words muffled.

Cecil leaped aside in time to avoid a stuffed seabag dropped by the swinging pirates, and trailed after Gretchen, reluctantly leaving his bone behind. He turned a corner and saw her approach a large man who, from the looks of him, had to be the captain. The man wore a long green coat and a black hat with a feather sticking out from one side and tall boots up to his thighs. He dropped down on one knee to greet Gretchen, stroking her head and speaking to her quietly as she placed the blue stone carefully into his other open palm. Cecil trotted toward them to make his introduction, but the captain stood quickly, slipping the stone into his pocket.

"Who let this mangy fat fellow on board?" the captain growled, glaring down at Cecil. "We have a cat. We don't need another." He struck Cecil with the side of his tall boot and sent him tumbling head over tail across the deck.

Cecil rolled onto his feet and crouched. *What*

was that *for?* he thought angrily. *These pirates are nuts!*

Gretchen sprang past him. "This way," she hissed, and Cecil followed, his mind whirling. *So the stones* are *worth something,* he thought. He felt anxious about the glowing white beauty he had brought with him, still hidden in the knothole. At least, he hoped it was still there. Would Gretchen help him get on the captain's good side? *Whatever happens,* Cecil thought, *that stone is my ticket. I'd better use it well.*

※ ※ ※

Cecil followed Gretchen among the kegs, barrels, crates, and seamen's legs on deck to the narrow steps that led down into the galley. At the second step she stopped and looked up at a porthole, which was set into the low slanted ceiling overhead. It struck Cecil as an odd place to put a window.

"Come sit here," she said, motioning him to her side. "And tell me what you see." He stepped down toward her, his eyes up on the porthole. The only thing he could see through it was a set of dark steps that seemed to lead down into darkness. But that was impossible because he knew there was nothing out there but the wide, flat deck.

"Is it a picture?" Cecil asked uncertainly.

Gretchen watched him with amusement. "What do you think?" she asked. "Move over this way. Take another look."

Cecil sat beside her and looked up at the glass. He gasped and stared openmouthed. Two cats sitting side by side were looking down at him through the porthole. He didn't recognize one of them, but the other had a most distinctive face. "That's you!" he cried, pointing at the smaller one with white and black fur. "Did someone paint you?" he asked, impressed.

Gretchen shook her head. "It's me, but not a painting," she said mysteriously. "Who's that other guy?"

Cecil studied the other cat. He was a big fellow with sparkling golden eyes and black fur with white whiskers. He looked kind of unkempt and reckless, and quite well-fed. Cecil liked the looks of him, actually.

"Well, *he* must be some sort of . . ." but he broke off, noticing with a shock that the big cat in the porthole had *also* raised his paw to point. "What's going on here?" he asked, as he and the porthole cat moved their paws up and down in sync.

"It's you!" laughed Gretchen. "It's a glass that shows you yourself. I think they call it a 'meer.' Isn't it funny? *This* is how I know what I look like."

Cecil began to understand. "That's . . . me?" he asked hesitantly. He straightened up and the porthole cat's face came closer. He put on his most menacing expression, holding up a paw and popping out his claws. *Hmmm, not bad.* He tried a knowing grin, and then a mischievous glance. *Nice!*

Gretchen rolled her eyes. "Okay. Come on, Mr. Full of Yourself, we've got to move. They'll be bringing stuff down here soon, and there's something else I want to show you." She turned back toward the deck. Cecil sent himself a regretful farewell salute in the porthole and followed her. No sooner were their feet on the deck than a crewman stomped up and kicked a barrel he was pushing onto its side. The cats sprang away and the sailor rolled the barrel noisily down the steps.

"Over here!" called Gretchen, leading the way. Cecil sprinted after her, suddenly finding himself balanced precariously on the bowsprit, a long thin spar jutting out over the water on the very front of the ship. "Come out a little farther," she suggested.

"We're out of the way here." She promptly began cleaning her tail, seemingly oblivious to the waves directly below.

Cecil edged out a few more inches, then settled his girth as best he could on the narrow spar. Looking down at the sea in the orange light of the sunset, he noticed the figure of a fabulous creature carved under the bow, in the same space where the two little girls had been on Anton's ship, the *Mary Anne*. This figure had a cat's face, surrounded by a magnificent circle of fur, and deep, wide eyes that appeared brave and wise.

"Amazing, huh?" asked Gretchen, following his gaze. "They call this ship the *Leone*. I've never seen a cat like that."

Cecil sat silently. The figurehead had brought Anton back to his mind, *where he should always be, if I'm ever going to find him,* thought Cecil reproachfully. Gretchen seemed to read his thoughts.

"Have you had any news yet about Anton?" she asked. "Have you picked up his trail at all?"

Cecil looked pained. "Nope." He sighed. "No idea where he is now. But . . ." He glanced up at her. "There have been a few strange signs, I guess."

"Like what?" she asked, stretching out her front paws along the bowsprit and sharpening her claws on the sides.

"Well, this will sound crazy," he said, "but I'm sure there's a huge and very old whale following me. Don't know what he's up to." He squinted off at the horizon. "And I've heard now a couple of times about some 'eye' up in the sky, and also a saying where one eye meets another eye." He shook his head and sighed again in frustration.

Gretchen sat up slowly and looked fixedly at Cecil. "An eye, yes," she said softly, as if talking to herself. "I've heard the saying, too, from Billy and my grandmother back in the village." She looked at the sky and her voice rose a little. "I think I saw it once—it's kind of misty, white and glowing, shining down on you in such a comforting way. And it tells you things, important things, without using words. You just get a feeling . . ."

Cecil looked up, too, but the slate blue sky was thick with muddy clouds, even covering the rising moon. "What feeling?" he asked quietly.

She paused and looked down again before speaking. "It . . . it told me to take heart, find my way back," she said. She nodded slightly and continued. "My grandmother told me the legend. She and Billy are the only ones who still remember it. Do you know my grandmother Mildred?"

"Sure, I've seen her," said Cecil. "But what *is* the legend? My mother never told us."

"It's an old cats' tale," Gretchen said, looking out over the waves, her gray eyes dark in the dusky light. She spoke softly. "The legend is that long ago, when cats began to be stolen from their homes and families and impressed into service on ships, there was no one to look after them. One young and kindhearted cat had been impressed by a crew that traveled through all of the widest oceans, and after many years and many voyages, he became old and very wise in the ways of ships and sailors. When the old cat's ship sank in a terrible storm and he drowned, the spirit protectors of the world pulled him from the depths of the ocean and sent him into the sky. And now his eye watches over all lost cats at sea."

"Huh," said Cecil, resting his chin on his front paws. "You believe this story?"

"I don't know," Gretchen said thoughtfully. "I'd

like to believe it." She briefly rubbed a paw over one ear. "Anyway, there's more."

Cecil swished his tail from side to side. "How much more?"

"Just a little," said Gretchen. "My grandmother also says there is a messenger in the ocean, some sort of creature who serves the spirit in the sky, protecting lost cats and helping them find their way home."

"What kind of creature? Like a fish?" asked Cecil, thinking of all the fish he'd devoured recently.

Gretchen shook her head. "No one knows. But the saying goes: Where the eye sees the eye, the lost shall be found."

Cecil lifted his head. "Well, Anton's lost."

Gretchen opened her eyes wide. "You are, too."

"And let's not forget *you,* right?" Cecil countered. "We're all three of us lost and far from home. But two of us are together now. So that's a start."

Gretchen gave him a wondering look and nodded. "That's true," she agreed.

The sudden rattle of heavy chains against the deck boards startled them, and Cecil struggled briefly to hang on to the spar as they glanced over to the deck. The crewmen moved purposefully now, tying down loose items and arranging the rigging. They were departing.

"Quick, come on!" called Gretchen, and she took one long leap, hurdling Cecil and landing expertly on the deck railing before dashing away. *Impressive,* thought Cecil. He turned precariously and followed at a gallop, trying to keep her in sight. He didn't know what she would do next; he liked that about her. But she had agreed that two might be better than one, so he made up his mind to trust her.

✤ ✤ ✤

Cecil dragged the small red bag from its hiding place, stepped into the side room with Gretchen, and dropped the bag on the floor. He pressed on the silk cloth with his paws until the white stone rolled out onto the floor between them and lay glowing faintly in the torchlight streaming in through the open doorway. Cecil looked at it and back at Gretchen. She looked at him and down at the stone.

"I stole this from the captain of my ship," Cecil

said evenly, watching her face. "I thought I might give it to your captain. Maybe he'll quit kicking me."

Gretchen seemed bewildered. "Yes, he'd be pleased, I'm sure, but . . ." Her face clouded over and she stood up. "Why didn't you tell me about this when you first got here?"

Cecil took a big breath and let it out again. He didn't know what to say.

"You thought I'd take it," she said slowly. "You thought I'd steal it and give it to the captain myself, didn't you?"

Cecil shifted uncomfortably and looked away. "Well, you might have," he said. "I don't know, you still could. You seem to like being the only cat aboard!"

Gretchen stared at him. "Do you know how lonely it is being the only cat aboard?" she asked quietly.

"Yeah, actually, I do," Cecil replied, standing to face her. "And it's awful, and I'd rather stay here." His eyes dropped to the white stone. "But it's kind of up to you now, isn't it?"

There was a long silence. They both sat down, carefully arranging their tails. Gretchen looked at him. Cecil knew that she was the quicker cat, that she could easily grab the stone and run. He knew he had to wait for her to choose his future. And he knew that she knew this as well. But his face remained perfectly peaceful, his golden eyes just barely smiling at her.

Finally, Gretchen smiled back. "Come on, ship-mate," she said with a sigh at last. "Bring your stone. There's someone you need to meet." She turned to the door.

Cecil picked up the stone in his mouth once more and together they walked, their tails in the air, to the captain's quarters.

CHAPTER 11

A Mouse at Sea

As Anton jumped down to the deck of the new ship, the clacker feathers lodged around his shoulders pricked him as he moved, and though he couldn't see them, he had a mental image of what he must look like. A cat with feathers! Approaching him was something he had rarely met on land, but never at sea: a toddling baby girl. Behind her came another onboard first for Anton: a young woman, presumably the child's mother, hurrying along with her hands on her hips, speaking in a way that made it clear she wanted to be listened to but didn't expect to be. The child had spotted Anton and was cooing joyfully, reaching out to grab him if she could, but Anton made sure she couldn't. He didn't want to hurt her, so he dodged this way and that, which made the baby laugh, and the mother laughed, too.

Anton sighed, leaping atop a coiled rope, thinking about how lonely it was on a ship, because the only creatures to talk to were rats, and they said nothing worth hearing. Anton's conversation with Dave the lizard had been the most companionable one he'd had in a long time. He thought of the long evening chats with Cecil, as they strolled about trading stories they had heard from other cats. Sometimes Anton had talked with some of the gulls that hung around the wharf, but it was hard to understand them and they were very full of themselves. Seen it all; that was gulls. He'd spoken to a dog occasionally. As Cecil pointed out, they weren't all bad, but one didn't see them much and they were often on leashes, which looked dreadful as far as Anton was concerned, though the dogs seemed quite happy with their lot. This baby could scarcely make her mother understand her, so there wouldn't be much hope there. "Cat," the baby crowed. "Cat."

The mother said, "Yes, that's a cat." They were both smiling and the mother approached Anton cautiously, holding out her hand for him to sniff. "How on earth did you get here?" she said. "And what bird have you tangled with? You must have dropped out of the sky."

She might pull the feathers off, Anton thought. She was very interested in them. He sat still and put on his most serious expression. She brought her fingers around his face cautiously, molding his cheek in her palm, and he felt such a chill run down his spine that he shrugged a little. She murmured something consoling. Then she began to feel around the base of the feathers. "I see," she said. "I see." Carefully she began to pluck them out one by one. Anton thought of his own mother, cleaning his face and neck with her rough pink tongue, but always gentle, even when she had to use her teeth to loosen up a knot of fur. He was so tired from his ordeal with the clackers that he nearly fell asleep while the woman petted and plucked and crooned to him. It was a good thing, he decided, to have a woman on a ship.

When the kind lady had removed his feather dressing, Anton set to work giving himself a good cleaning from head to toe. The captain had come out by this time and spoke with his wife, who gestured from Anton to the sea, to the sky, and back again. The captain puffed his pipe, wide-eyed at first, then squinting closely at Anton, he picked up a feather from the pile on the deck, looked up at the sky, and examined the feather as if it was a text. "A cat that falls out of the sky is one we'd better make welcome," he said. Taking up the baby, who shouted with joy, he carried her off to the cabin. His wife, with a nod at Anton that told him he was on his own, followed her family.

There were sailors aloft in the rigging, and one fellow working on a barrel near the stern. Anton could smell fish cooking in the fo'c'sle. He leaped down from the rope coil and slunk along toward the promising odor.

The moment he stepped through the doorway, Anton knew there was a mouse behind the hardtack barrel, but he had to pay attention to the humans who greeted his appearance with shouts of surprise. "Will you look at what the cat drug in," one shouted to the next. And another said, "It's a catfish for sure." The cook, a young fellow with bright blue eyes and a black beard that grew to his chest, studied Anton with a suspicious look, but Anton sat down and sniffed the air so appreciatively that the cook's expression softened, and he said something that contained two words Anton knew well: "yer dinner." It wasn't long before the traditional tin pan of the sea galley was put before him, and a meaty fish head stared back balefully at the new ship's cat.

The next morning Anton took a long stroll on the deck, allowing the news of his arrival to be passed from mouth to ear all up and down the length of the ship. He noted a few good spots for snoozing in the sun and others for hiding from bad weather, or that baby. The sailors weighed anchor and dropped the mainsail, which took the breeze at once. The ship began to plow smoothly through the calm sea, steering away from the island. Going where?

As the sun descended into the horizon, pouring a stream from a flaming red cauldron into the darkening water, Anton made his way back to the fo'c'sle to deal with the mouse hiding behind the barrel. The sailors had finished their meals and were either sleeping or on deck, and the cook had shut down the stove for the night. Anton didn't bother with a stealthy approach; his nose told him exactly where the mouse was. He walked to the back of the barrel and shoved his head into the space where it curved away from the wall.

The mouse let out a shriek and shrunk down on the floor, hiding his head between his front feet. "I knew it," he cried. "I knew it. Now I'll be eaten, just like my poor father and my brother, and there's no escape." And then he sat up, tears streaming from his eyes, his nose running hope-lessly, shivering from his ears to his tail. "Please don't eat me," he said through his sobs. "I'm barely a morsel to you, but to myself, I'm all I have left. I'm the last mouse in my family."

"That's an interesting argument," Anton said.

The mouse pulled his tail round and used the tip to wipe the tears from his eyes. "You don't mean it," he said. "That's the teasing way of you heart-less felines. Soon you'll be tossing me from paw to paw just for the sport of seeing a poor wee beastie in terror." His tail was of no use against the steady flow of his tears and he let it go. "I'll not run wild for your amusement," he said, looking sullen, but still the tears poured down his face and his shoul-ders shuddered. "My dear brother did that, and to no avail."

"You need to stop blubbering or you're going to drown in your own tears," Anton warned.

"Would that I could," the mouse replied.

What an odd mouse, Anton thought. Rodents weren't generally thoughtful, and rats, as Anton recalled too well, were downright murderous. "So, you were close to your brother?"

"We were different as night and day," the mouse said. "Nobody would have taken us for brothers. He was a big mouse, and he had a fine, dark pelt, and he loved adventures, whereas I was always"—and here he sniffed and wiped his nose with the back of his front foot—"I was always what you see before you. But we were close. Oh, he was my dearest friend. We were close like that." The mouse held up his foot and somehow managed to cross the two front claws.

"I have a brother like that," Anton said. Cecil appeared for a moment in his mind's eye, just as if he were there before him, and Anton sighed as he looked back at the still sniveling mouse.

"That's fine for you," the mouse said. "Nobody has eaten your brother."

"What was his name?" Anton asked.

"Oh, lord of mice, what do you care what my

poor dead brother's name is? Just finish me off and be done with it, will you not?"

"I'm going to tell you something that will surprise you," Anton said. "I don't really like the taste of mice."

"Right, shipmate. I'm sure you don't. You're just making the sacrifice for the good of the enterprise."

"Well, that's just it. If the sailors find out, or that lady, if she finds out you're here, they won't feed me until I hand over your corpse. But if they don't know you're here and you're the only mouse on board . . ."

"I am that. The last of a fine clan."

"I'll bet you could find enough to eat without the humans noticing you're here."

"I'm a creature of great stealth and caginess. That's how I've outlived my poor family."

"Well, then. If no one sees you, I'm not obliged to kill you."

"Are you not?" said the mouse. "Are you not obliged by the ancient enmity between our kind?"

Anton chuckled. This mouse was a dramatic mouse. "What's your name?" he asked.

"My name is Hieronymus," the mouse said proudly. "My brother was Geronymus."

"Her-on-i-mus," Anton repeated. Even the mouse's name was funny. "My name is Anton."

"I can't say I'm pleased to meet you."

"Right," said Anton. "The ancient enmity."

"I won't deny that you're an improvement over the last cat on this ship."

"What happened to him?"

"He was a great brute, always getting himself into scrapes. Once, he got himself locked in the larder for two days. Would that they'd never found him. The ship got into some wicked weather and he was stupid enough to go aloft. A big wave came and pulled him off the ropes, dashed him on the deck, and before he could get to his feet, he was swept over the side into the deep blue sea."

Anton gasped. "Poor fellow," he said. "That's a terrible fate."

"Excuse me if I'm dry-eyed," said Hieronymus. "He ate my dear brother before my eyes, and not in one bite, either."

"Yes," Anton said. "That must have been traumatic for you."

"It was the worst moment of my life." And the mouse burst into tears again.

As Anton frowned at the mouse's fresh waterworks,

he felt a bit of moisture gather in his own eyes. Hieronymus had given him the thought that Cecil, who was so reckless, might have had some terrible accident back home, and Anton would have no way of knowing. "Please stop your crying," Anton said.

To his surprise the mouse nodded his head and said, between sobs, that he would try. When he could control his voice again, Hieronymus asked, "What's your brother's name?"

"Cecil," said Anton. "I got impressed on the wharf. He was far down the dock and I called to him from the ship, but I expect he couldn't hear me."

As he spoke there was a shout on the deck, and the sailors began to stir in their bunks. "Look," Anton said. "Just stay out of sight."

"You won't see me, unless you've a mind to," Hieronymus replied. "I generally stay here until the night watch goes on, and then I move out to that big rope coil up in the bow. I've a comfy nest there for sleeping, and if I can't sleep, I like to see the stars."

A stargazing mouse. Anton chuckled. He knew he'd come to a low pass to have taken a mouse for a friend, but Hieronymus was clearly a very unusual mouse.

In the days that followed, Anton established a routine on this new ship to which he had been delivered by a whale. It was much smaller than the *Mary Anne,* with a crew of only eight men, not counting the captain and his family. The captain's wife took an interest in Anton and invited him into the family's quarters, where she spent much of her time confined with the baby. Anton was wary of the baby, who charged at him on unsteady legs, but the lady was kind and offered Anton treats, a little milk in a saucer or a bit of meat or fish from her own plate. One day, when she found him curled up for a nap in a basket of clothes, she laughed, gently chasing him out. "You want a bed," she said. On his next visit, she showed him a wooden box with one end open, in which she had placed a soft cushion. *Now this is the life,* Anton thought, as he curled up for a good long snooze. The top of the box had slats that let in light and air, but the sides were solid, so he felt safe and secret, comfy and warm.

In the evenings, he visited the fo'c'sle for his dinner, after which he went out on the deck for a stroll, ending, when the night watch came on, with a visit to the rope coil in the prow and a conversation with Hieronymus the mouse. And could

that mouse talk. He was a well-traveled, observant, witty, and lyrical mouse, a spinner of tales full of adventure, bravery, and narrow escapes. Many of his stories had been handed down in his family: the story of Great-Uncle Pyramus, who fell asleep in what he thought was an oversize basket and woke up high above the earth in a hot-air balloon; of Great-Grampa Maximus, who was making a nest in a wheat field when out of the woods came hordes of furious humans marching in long lines toward one another and firing rifles, charging and falling and firing until the air was all smoke, and the ground so thickly covered with the dead and dying that Maximus nearly drowned in a pool of blood; of cousin Minimus, who wound up somewhere miles inland and set up house in a big seashell because he loved to hear the sea when he was falling asleep; and of his own uncle Micromus, who, having perfected the art of springing traps with his tail, died suddenly when he bit into a brightly colored wire he thought might be useful for pulling free the cheese once the trap was sprung. Hieronymus was also revealed to be a thoughtful mouse. He had theories about why all animals could understand each other while humans could only talk to other humans, and why rocks sank if they fell off ships, but ships didn't sink if you put rocks in them.

Hieronymus wasn't a bad listener, either. Anton told him about his adventures since he'd left home, about the vicious birds and about how he came to the ship on a whale. One evening he told the mouse about the eye he'd seen in the sky, most recently with Dave. "Do you know the expression, 'Where the eye sees the eye, the lost shall be found'?"

"Can't say as I do. Is the eye a cat's eye?" Hieronymus asked.

"It does look like a cat's eye."

"We have a different expression for that sky. We say, 'Cat's eye in the sky, a mouse will soon die.'"

"No, really?" said Anton.

"But I saw that eye once, with my dear father, and he said there was an old legend attached to it that came from before there were even cats in the world."

"There were no cats in the world?" Anton said wonderingly.

"No, nor mice either. Just fish for some reason. But this eye protects cats; it's special to them. That's why no other animals eat them. No such luck for us mice. We must have been created by a very careless fellow indeed."

"The clackers were going to eat me," observed Anton.

"Well, in those days, when cats were new, they were really, really big. Now they're a lot smaller. When humans started taking them to sea, the eye followed to watch over them, and it still watches them and protects them."

Anton puzzled over this information. A world without cats—he couldn't make sense of that.

The ship sailed on through good weather and bad, and the routine of the sailors hardly varied. We must be going somewhere, Anton thought. We can't just sail forever. But whenever he looked out from the prow, the sea stretched out endlessly. He imagined Cecil raiding a crab party or boring everyone back home with his tales of schooner triumphs. How Anton would love to hear one of those stories right now.

Then, one morning, something extraordinary happened.

All the humans simply disappeared.

CHAPTER 12

Trade Winds

I n his new life on the pirate ship, Cecil found himself with quite a lot to do. Birds who landed on deck had to be chased off, as they made a terrible mess. If they perched up in the rigging, which they often did to taunt the cats below with cruel and tasteless jokes, then Cecil climbed the maze of ropes attached to the masts to reach them. Mice and rats who sneaked on board during raids had to be disposed of one way or another. And there was a surprising variety of beetles, worms, and spiders to be caught, batted into submission, and devoured; most of these were

179

imported in the food and loot taken from other vessels. Cecil relished his duties, though once he was stung by what he thought was a small crab until Gretchen called it a scorpion, and his paw swelled up to a painful and tremendous size.

Then there was the actual business of pirating, spurts of furious activity for the crew in the midst of long periods of idleness. Sometimes the target ship fought back, its great guns lobbing heavy balls of iron over to the pirate ship, where they landed randomly and sometimes did severe damage. During these occasions the cats found it best to scamper belowdecks and hide. Cecil learned to keep his guard up most of the time, since a passing crewman was just as likely to give a kick of the boot as he was a friendly pat, and one had to keep that knowledge foremost in one's mind as a ship's cat.

One bright day when Cecil and Gretchen were dozing back to back in the sun on the roof of the map room, a pirate approached suddenly, scooped them up, and dropped them neatly into a crate, banging the lid shut with a mallet. Cecil sprang to his feet, yowling as he pushed frantically on the sides of the crate, to no avail. He ran in tight circles wildly until he noticed Gretchen just sitting, an expression of displeasure on her face. He stopped yowling and faced her. "Hey," he said, breathing heavily. "Why aren't you trying to get out of here?"

She shrugged in resignation, looking moodily out through the slats of the crate. "They've done this sort of thing before. It means we're headed into a port, and they don't want us wandering off."

"Really? A port?" Cecil asked. He looked out as well, and sure enough spotted a dark lump of land in the distance, growing steadily wider. "This could be my chance," he said, mostly to himself. "Maybe I'll finally get some news about Anton."

Gretchen examined the pads of her front paw. "I hope so," she said.

The pirates had replaced the red pirate flags with less threatening blue-and-white striped ones, and once the ship was tied up at the dock they stomped down the gangplanks in high spirits. The sailor carrying the cat crate brought it to a side street set up with colorful stalls and strewn with chattering brown-skinned people. The air was warm and moist, and the only shade came from odd trees that had all their leaves bursting out at the top. Cecil and Gretchen's crate was placed on

top of another in the midst of a group of cages and boxes, each holding a creature of some kind. Some of the creatures turned to look at them with interest; others ignored them. The two cats huddled together in the back of the crate.

"I was afraid of this," whispered Gretchen. "They call this the 'markit.'"

"What's that?" asked Cecil, his eyes darting all around.

"People come to trade, you know, give something and get something else in return. The pirates love trading."

"What's that got to do with *us*?" Cecil asked, looking at Gretchen nervously, but she only nodded grimly toward the man in the center of the cages. He was speaking rapidly to a strangely dressed sailor, handing him a box with three small turtles inside in exchange for a handful of brightly colored beads. "Oh," said Cecil softly, slumping down. "Trading." He turned to Gretchen again and whispered fiercely, "I thought they *liked* us!"

She shook her head. "They like silver more."

Cecil glared through the slats. "*Now* you tell me."

The cats could still see the ship from their stall, and they watched in grudging fascination as the pirate crew circulated among many people on the waterfront, talking and gesturing, laughing and arguing. Each sailor seemed to have with him a pouch on a string containing items stolen on raids. They made exchanges with men from the town, who gave them back different items—bottles of liquid, knives or swords, or small pieces of round, flat, shiny metal. Gretchen remarked that these last were what they called "silver," and the sailors valued them highly, privately counting and stacking them over and over. Cecil saw the captain himself offering the glowing white stone Cecil had brought on board in exchange for a very long cutlass, its blade flashing in the sun.

The cats spoke to the other creatures near them, asking about Anton, the whale, the legend. Several seagulls perched on top of the stall swore they had seen the whale surfacing here and there, though Gretchen later discounted their story, as seagulls, she maintained, were notorious liars. An almond-eyed ferret recited the expression while standing on his hind legs in his cage, his skinny arms outstretched: "Where the eye sees the eye, the lost shall be found." None of the others had more than that to offer.

"Thank you so much," said Cecil to each, his spirits gradually falling.

No one had seen or even heard of Anton. An unnaturally large and menacing bird caged on the far side of the stall had been entirely focused on a small lemur in the crate just below it all day, clacking its beak repeatedly and muttering.

"That's a vulture," Gretchen said.

"Wow," said Cecil wryly. "You really know your avian classification."

When a sailor traded for the vulture and set it on his shoulder, held there by a chain attached to its ankle, it looked at Cecil, nodded its head, and croaked, "*Agggk*. Dinner." As its new owner strolled off, it swayed its huge ugly head from side to side cryptically.

Cecil gulped and turned away. "Did you see the beak on that thing?" he asked Gretchen shakily.

"Don't worry about it," said Gretchen. "They only eat stuff that's already dead."

Whenever an interested trader passed the stall and looked in at them, the cats sprawled on their backs with their eyes half-closed, trying to look as unappealing as possible. Life was tolerable on the pirate ship—at least they had enough to eat—and they didn't want to be separated at this point. Also, Cecil thought, if he got stuck on land he might never find Anton. So they tried their best not to be traded. During one of these episodes, as they lay stiffly in the crate, a low, rough voice spoke to them from very close by.

"You're not fooling anyone, you know. You don't look nearly bad enough."

Cecil and Gretchen lifted their heads and focused their eyes on a large golden-haired dog peering into the crate, tail wagging and pink tongue lolling. The cats stood and took a few steps backward.

Gretchen seemed unable to speak, so Cecil responded. "Hey there, have we met?"

"Name's Remy," said the dog happily. He was tall and muscular, with floppy ears and long, rippling fur. Cecil noticed that he wore a red headscarf tied around his neck. *That looks so stylish,* thought Cecil, though in the next moment he realized that some human must have put it on him. Then he thought the dog just looked like a clown.

"Are you being traded?" Cecil asked.

Remy woofed a short laugh, causing Gretchen

to flinch. "Not a chance," he said. "I'm with him," and he gestured with his black nose back over his shoulder toward the market master. As he did so, the cats spotted a leather collar circling his neck, tucked under the scarf.

"So," said Gretchen, regaining her voice and stepping forward. "You're not . . . free. Right? That man owns you?"

Remy chuckled again as his deep brown eyes appraised the crate. "More free than *you*, eh? We don't get that many cats in here; usually they're pretty well-liked by their owners. Were you no good at your job on the ship?" He seemed genuinely interested.

"We were *great*," replied Gretchen pointedly, arching her back. "But it's a crew of pirates . . ."

Remy nodded and smiled. "Gotcha."

A small gray monkey began shrieking hysterically in a cage across from the cats. In a flash the dog darted to the monkey's cage and issued several sharp barks and one long growl, frightening the monkey into cowering silence. Remy trotted back and sat next to the cats' crate.

"Not bad," said Cecil quietly.

"I'm good at my job," said Remy.

"He's not going to let us out of here, if that's why you're flattering him," Gretchen murmured to Cecil. Remy woofed in agreement.

"Okay," said Cecil, "then have you seen any large old whales around here by chance? Or a mysterious eye, up in the sky?"

Remy snorted. "Whales don't usually pull up to the dock to visit, so that's a big no," he said. "As for an eye . . ." He paused, panting. "A couple of nights ago I did see something like that. A bright cloud, could have been a trick of the moonlight. I'm not sure."

Gretchen stepped up to the front of the crate and pressed her face against the slats. "Did it speak to you? Do you remember any more?"

"It passed over me, blew right by. But there was one odd thing about it," he said, staring at Gretchen's face. "It looked just like *your* eye."

A dreadful squawking rose from a cage down the row containing a fearsome white-headed bird. It had beaten its wings against the cage door until the thin reeds gave way, and now the bird stumbled out, furious, its sharp beak slashing the air. Remy leaped and in one motion brought the bird to the ground, firmly but carefully and without crushing it. The market master rushed over and wrestled the bird into another cage as Remy stepped back.

Cecil noticed a deep scratch on the dog's foreleg from the bird's beak and felt his heart pound. In a strange way he envied that scratch. Even though Remy was "owned," he was free to run away if he wanted to; he was in charge of his own destiny. Cecil, at this point, felt his freedom slipping away.

That evening as the pirate ship left port and sailed smoothly out on the dark open sea, Cecil, though relieved he and Gretchen had not been traded, was quietly miserable. He wondered how many other ports there were like that one, and whether Anton could have gotten off his ship at one of them and started a new life in a village somewhere, giving up the idea of getting home. How could Cecil find him then? Or worse—the encounter with the vulture was the first time he had reckoned with the idea that Anton might not even be alive anymore.

"Where are you, brother?" he said softly to the horizon.

Gretchen crouched next to him on a box by the deck rail, not knowing what to say. She could not say that it would all work out in the end, because at this point, she didn't see how it would. So she curled her tail carefully around behind him and sat silently, watching the empty ocean and the wide starless sky, waiting with him for a sign.

❖ ❖ ❖

Days and nights went by without sighting a single other ship or land of any kind. This was quite unusual, and the crew of the *Leone* began to get restless. There was some concern over the supply of fresh water on board, and indeed whether they had fallen off course somehow. The captain strode up and down the deck, growling at his men as they took measurements by the weak sun and consulted charts and maps. The stars, their usual steadfast guide, were obscured by swirling clouds night after night until the crewmen threw up their hands, helpless. Pointing up at the sun and then straight off the starboard side, the captain barked an order to head in that direction, but the wind was so light that the sails barely caught enough to turn the ship.

Gretchen and Cecil tried to escape the late afternoon heat under the shelter of a canvas tarp.

"I mean," said Cecil, exasperated, "the saying is,

'Where the eye *sees* the eye,' right? So: that's two eyes. I think one of the eyes has to be the one in the sky, from the legend."

"Definitely," agreed Gretchen, nodding. "The shape *is* a cat's eye, just like the dog said."

Cecil thought again about the warm glow he'd felt on the clipper.

"But what's the other eye?" she asked. "That's the question."

"Could it be *my* eye?" he wondered, touching his paw to the side of his face. "Or the eye of any creature who's in trouble?"

Gretchen frowned. "I don't think so. When I saw it, nothing in particular happened to me. I wasn't 'found.' And the dog said he saw it, their eyes met, but he didn't say that anything happened to him, either."

"Hmmm," said Cecil, scratching behind his left ear thoughtfully. "So what is . . . the second eye?"

At that moment they both felt a subtle but unmistakable lift and fall of the ship, which was odd after so many days of stillness. The two cats emerged from under the tarp and hopped up on a barrel near the stern to survey the situation, which was strange indeed. The sky was the color of swirling smoke and the sea was a dark gray-green, with small ripples beginning to appear on the surface. Peering over the railing, they saw little fish moving in fast schools under the ship, and birds flying singly in all directions just above the water. "Birds usually mean there's land nearby," Gretchen said, "but there's nothing to see from here."

The crew behaved as if they were suspicious of the weather, scowling at the sky and sea. The wind whipped unpredictably, snapping the sails taut and plunging the ship in one direction, then dying just as suddenly, then changing direction. Sheets of rain passed over them like waves with brief periods of calm in between.

"What's going on? Where are we?" asked Cecil, trying to take everything in at once.

"Don't know," replied Gretchen. "Never seen anything like this before. I don't like the looks of it, though."

In silent agreement, the cats remained on deck despite the intermittent soakings, huddled together for warmth and protection. They both felt that what happened next might be important somehow. The night passed slowly, as the strange weather neither worsened nor abated, yet seemed to be pulling the ship intentionally off course. The cats dozed, waking in the darkness to the sound of the wind blustering against the sails. Finally Cecil thought he detected through the gloom the barest brightening of the sky on the horizon. *Dawn must be coming at last,* he thought. He had just noticed a bird flying by both backward and upside down when a pirate shouted from high in the crow's nest. All eyes looked up at him, and then to where he was pointing.

Gretchen got to her feet. "Land," she said.

Cecil stood as well and squinted into the dim light. Directly off the bow, though still a good distance off, was a tall green island. Almost pointed at the top, with steeply sloping sides, the land appeared to be covered with lush vegetation and small trees, but no ships, houses, or other signs of people that Cecil could see.

"That's odd, isn't it?" he asked. "The way it just . . . showed up?" He glanced at Gretchen.

"It wasn't there last night." She sounded faintly alarmed.

In the dawn haze as the sunlight played on vapors rising from the ground, the island glowed majestically. The thinning mist made it appear to be advancing rapidly toward them. The crew of the pirate ship now just stood and stared. Finally the captain, his large feathered hat set aside because of the unpredictable gusts of wind, gripped the railing to steady himself.

"Pull yourselves together, lads!" he shouted. "It's land we've been waiting for, is it not? And here we have it!" He gestured widely at the island. "Drop anchor and make ready a landing party to fetch water and whatever stores are to be had. On the double!"

As the crew broke out of their stupor and hurried to their tasks, the first mate, a short man with silver spectacles and a blue brocade vest, stood next to the captain looking out at the ocean, his spyglass held slack by his side.

"Cap'n, sir," he said in a low voice.

"What is it?" The captain whirled to him.

"The currents, do ye see?" He pointed. "An' the wind, too. We're bein' pushed."

"Well, of course we are, you fool!" the captain growled. "That's how we *sail*—currents and wind—is it not?" He picked up his feathered hat and swatted the first mate's head with it.

"I only mean, sir," said the first mate, flinching,

"this time it seems we're being drawn in, like a magnet's pulling at us, in a manner of speakin'."

The captain stared. Indeed, the ship felt like it was moving on its own, turning to starboard, then to port, as puffs of wind and surges of waves drew it along a path into the island, while no man's hand touched the wheel. When the ship closed to within a few hundred yards of the shoreline, the wind died and the waves became calm. The ship slowed to a halt, turning lazily in place.

The captain glanced sharply around. "What's this now?"

Pointing this way and that with his long cutlass, he ordered the sails trimmed to bring the ship around, but there was no breeze to catch no matter what the crew tried. Finally he stomped his boot on the deck, chose six crewmen with a whip of his sword and ordered them into the dinghy.

Cecil turned to watch the sailors. "Now what are they doing?" he asked Gretchen.

"They're going to try to send a small boat out to it," she replied, glancing at the preparations. "It's weird. I think the crew is scared."

The cats turned toward the bow again and Gretchen gasped sharply.

"Cecil!" she called. "There it is!"

It was the Eye.

Suspended low in the thin gray clouds directly above the island, it glowed faintly but steadily. Cecil stood frozen, captured by the sight.

"It does look like a cat's eye, doesn't it?" he said admiringly. "But why do you suppose it's over *there*?" The crew seemed not to have noticed it.

Gretchen suddenly had a thought, blazing like a flame in her mind. She shoved Cecil with both front paws. "You've got to go there. Get on that little boat right now." She was practically bulldozing him with her head. "I don't know why the Eye is there and I don't know why we seem to be heading in that direction or why the men are acting strange, but it must mean something, and you need to get closer."

Cecil nodded energetically. "Sounds like an adventure to me."

"Just go," Gretchen insisted.

They scrambled toward the gap in the railing where the small boat was being lowered into the water, but the men standing on deck brushed them back with their boots.

"I'll distract them," called Gretchen. "Jump!"

She immediately fell flat on her back and began such a horrific yowling that Cecil thought she had actually been hurt. The pirates looked over at the writhing cat for a moment.

Oh! thought Cecil. *Got it,* and he wove between the legs of the men until he reached the gap. It was a long way down, and the boat was already full with the six men. *I'll break all my bones jumping in there,* he thought, but he was out of time as they were taking up the oars to row. He did the next best thing he could think of. He missed.

And for the second time in his life, he was rescued from the waves by a human. The first mate with the spectacles and the blue vest fished Cecil out of the ocean and dropped him into the boat under the tip of the prow, where he curled into a miserable, wet, salty ball of cat.

"Shoulda let it drown, I say," grumbled one of the pirates, glaring at the bedraggled cat.

"Ah, you never know," returned the spectacled man mildly. "He may find somethin' interestin', he may. Besides, black's a lucky color, ay?" He pointed to Cecil's soaked fur and smiled.

✤ ✤ ✤

After rowing halfway to the island in the choppy sea, the men in the dinghy were aghast to see it begin to split apart. They dropped their oars and stared, until they realized that it was not one island, but two; the larger one was closer and another smaller one was just behind the first. The wind and waves had risen again and were nudging the small boat to the west bit by bit, so they could not seem to reach the first island. When the second came into view it gave the impression that the two were drifting apart.

"What the devil is this nonsense?" cried one of the men.

Cecil was watching as well, holding on to the prow of the boat with his paws. He felt a strange tingle at the tip of his tail and inside his ears. He had no idea what the pirates would do now, but he could still see the Eye, steadily glowing above the islands.

Like the pages of a great book falling slowly open, the parting islands separated, and in the channel between them, on water as placid as blue glass, an unexpected sight was revealed.

It was a ship.

CHAPTER 13

Adrift

The morning light streamed through the skylight of the captain's cabin as Anton woke from a deep sleep in the snug crate the captain's wife had prepared for his bed. When he stepped out, he noticed the cabin door standing open, the baby's toys scattered across the floor, but no sound of voices from the deck or footsteps in the gangway, no sound at all. The breakfast dishes lay half empty on the table, and the teapot stood ready on the sideboard.

Anton hurried up the steps to the deck. Only a

few sails were set and no sailors were climbing in the rigging or working on the deck. Were they all in the fo'c'sle? He sprinted the length of the ship and down into the galley. The stove was warm, the air smelled of coffee, the tin pans were stacked in the rack near the long table where the sailors took their meals, but there was not a soul in the place, not in the galley or in the bunks that lined the walls. Where was everybody? Were they hiding?

Hieronymus appeared at the galley door. "They're gone," he said.

"Is it some kind of joke?" Anton exclaimed. "Where could they go?"

"I don't know," the mouse replied. "I've been searching all morning."

Anton pushed past the mouse back to the deck. "Is there land nearby? Maybe they went ashore?"

"I don't see any land. But you take a look. Your eyes are better than mine."

Anton leaped up to a spar and climbed until he had a good view in all directions. Nothing but sea, sea, sea. No boat, large or small, in sight. The wind picked up, filling the few sails that were before it and the ship plunged through the waves, but it wavered without a helmsman and the sails drooped and then filled again. They were adrift, a cat and a mouse, in an abandoned ship.

"What do we do now?" Anton said to Hieronymus when he came down from the ropes.

"Find something to eat and drink," said the mouse.

"That's easy," Anton replied. "They left breakfast on the table. It's that oatmeal stuff you like so much."

"That's good news," the mouse allowed. "But what do we do after that?"

After that they searched the ship from one end to the other and found that every morsel of food and drop of water was stored away in barrels or cans or jars or metal boxes. They tried knocking the jars off shelves. Anton pried at tin lids with his claws. They spent several hours trying to break into one of the tins Anton knew contained the delicious bony little fish he had sometimes sampled. "It's just too frustrating," he said, flipping the can against the stove. "I know those fish are in there."

Hieronymus nodded, looking serious. "What we need most is water," he said. "I had an uncle who died of thirst in a larder full of flour."

"I'm thirsty right now," Anton agreed.

The water barrel was in the galley, sealed by a heavy lid with wire latches on two sides. Anton stood on the top pulling at the latches, but to no avail. Hieronymus ran all around the edges, then leaped to the floor. He stood on his hind legs and felt his way around the base with his forepaws.

"What are you looking for?" Anton said, jumping down beside him.

"A bowl," he said. "And I think I've found it."

It was really a slightly depressed area in the floorboard, no doubt worn by the cook's boots over the years, as he stood there lowering his big ladle into the bucket.

Anton poked his nose against the wood. "It's dry as a bone," he said. "What good will it do us?"

Hieronymus placed his front feet against the barrel just above the low spot in the floor. "I'm going to gnaw my way through right here." He sat back and bared his sharp little teeth. "I hope these hold up. How do they look?"

"Too small, is how they look," Anton replied. "It's impossible."

"Never say that," Hieronymus said fiercely. "What is a mouse designed for? I'll tell you. Getting into very small places and gnawing. Great-Granduncle Portymus gnawed his way out of a sealed coffin."

"This wood looks pretty hard to me," Anton observed.

Hieronymus sat up on his hind legs and pressed his cheek against the rough wood of the barrel. He closed his eyes and said solemnly, "I, Hieronymus, will gnaw a hole in this barrel. I swear by all that is sacred to the mouse I will not fail."

And then, without another word to Anton, the mouse bared his teeth again and began to gnaw at the wood. There was nothing to do but stand by and cheer him on. Hieronymus gnawed and gnawed, pausing repeatedly to spit out the bits of wood pulp he dislodged. He gnawed until the sun was high in the sky, but there was only a slight dent in the wood. He plopped down on his side. "I'll just rest a minute," he said.

Anton examined the barrel. "Maybe I can pull out these little slivers with my claws," he said, and he tried, but with little success. Hieronymus got to his feet and was back at it, gnaw, gnaw, gnaw. The dent widened and deepened and the mouse's nose disappeared inside it. When he stopped again, the dent was a real hole. "You're making progress," Anton said.

Hieronymus leaned against the barrel, picking little bits of wood from his teeth with the tiny claws of his forepaw. "My jaws hurt," he said, but more as an observation than a complaint.

"If only you could have something to drink," Anton said.

"Well," replied the mouse. "That's just the point, isn't it?" He returned to his labor.

The sun was sinking into the horizon, and Hieronymus was up to his neck in the barrel, when he braced his back legs against the side and carefully pulled himself free of the hole. He landed on his back on the floor, feet in the air, mouth open, eyes glazed. His mouth, nose, and chin were covered in blood.

Anton was horrified. "You've got to give up. You can't go on. You're bleeding. You need to rest."

Hieronymus looked up at him. "I don't have to go on," he said weakly. "Look at the barrel."

Anton bent down and put his face close to the tiny hole. The inside of it was pink with the mouse's blood. *Pink?* Anton thought. Then the pink turned pale and translucent. A drop of moisture formed at the edge of the opening and in the next moment, it ran down the side of the barrel to the floor. "You did it!" Anton exclaimed. "You gnawed all the way through the barrel!"

Mouse and cat sat watching a small pool of water gather in the shallow depression at the base of the barrel. Anton insisted Hieronymus have the first drink and he agreed, lapping at the thin film of moisture with his small, bloody tongue. He was content to rest while they waited for enough water to collect for Anton to have even a swallow. Licking water off a floor wasn't the best way to quench a thirst, but the slow drip from the bottom of the barrel guaranteed that they would be able to drink enough water to stay alive.

❊ ❊ ❊

Furred animals, Hieronymus reminded Anton, could go without food much longer than they could without water, but after three days with not a bite to eat, Anton had begun to think otherwise. He had given up trying to open tins and jars and even the champion gnawer Hieronymus admitted defeat. "They put the food in these things to thwart creatures like me," he said, pushing a tin of hard-tack across the floor. "It's diabolical."

Anton settled on deck in the hopes that a flying fish might pass over, or that a bird would perch in the rigging low enough to be swatted down. "There's nourishment to be had in chewing rope," Hieronymus suggested. "My mother told me that." But though rope might keep a mouse alive, Anton found he couldn't chew it properly.

"It just makes me thirstier," he said. Every few hours he went down to the larder to lap at the water trough. Each time he came up the steps, he felt a little weaker.

More days passed, with the ship ambling through the waves, listing this way and that, the sails occasionally filling for a goodish spell, but no land or other ship was ever in sight. The days got warmer, and the sun got bigger, until the two furred animals were forced to seek out shade on the deck. The sea changed from brown to blue, and the waves thinned out until the surface of the water was as smooth as glass. The ship floated upon it, the sails hanging limply from the spars, as still as if it were at anchor. Anton and Hieronymus slept all day and passed the night dozing fitfully, scanning the skies for some sign of life. Anton could barely raise himself to look over the prow, and he feared that if the longed-for fish or bird did appear, he would be too weak to catch it. "I feel muddled," he told Hieronymus. "I can't think straight."

One night Anton woke to the sound of human voices singing and a full moon bathing the still waters with pearly light. He lifted his head and sniffed the air. "What beautiful music," he said. Hieronymus, snoring mousily at the bottom of the coiled rope, didn't stir. Anton stretched his back legs, then arched his back, rousing himself, and made his way to the rail. What he saw made his jaw drop. The ship was surrounded by waves of glowing green grasses, swaying softly in the slight current of the water. It looked like electric seaweed! The voices seemed to come from out of the air, high and clear, singing a dreamy melody that made Anton feel, deep in his chest, something he hadn't felt in a long time: the first stirring of a purr.

"Oh, what is it?" he said. Then, toward the stern, he saw a pale hand moving among the glowing weeds, pulling something back and forth. Another hand appeared closer to the ship, and another farther to the prow, slowly, carefully pulling some-thing through the waving grasses. It reminded Anton of the captain's wife, sitting at her dressing table at night, sometimes humming to herself.

"It's a comb," he said. "They're combing their hair?" And now, here and there among the waving green islets, pale faces appeared, human children's faces, all with the same sea-green eyes and pink rose petal lips, singing blissfully in the warm night air, combing their sparkling tresses, which flashed streaks of phosphorescent light across the water's still surface. Anton stood gazing in fascination at the pretty, joyful creatures. One of the children near the ship looked at Anton, smiled, and waved his hand, as if to say fare-thee-well. Then, rais-ing his arms over his head, he dived down into the water.

Anton waved his paw back, leaning out over the rail to get a closer look. As the beautiful child slipped beneath the surface of the translucent sea, a big silvery fish tail flipped up behind him. One by one the strange night visitors turned from the ship and dived back into the sea, their voices fall-ing away, their dreamy human faces disappearing, followed by a cacophony of slapping sounds as their flashing silver tails propelled them down into the depths. Scarcely a minute later they were gone.

"This world is full of wonders," Anton said. He stepped back from the rail, savoring the sensation of amazement, which, while it lasted, took his mind off his hunger.

"It is indeed," said Hieronymus, who had come up behind him, rubbing his sleepy eyes with both his paws.

Anton took a step toward the hatch, but his back legs went out from under him and he fell on his side. "That marvelous singing," he said. "Those pretty children, with their fish tails. What a magical night."

"What children?" Hieronymus asked, eyeing his friend anxiously. "What singing? I didn't hear anything."

Anton groggily got to his feet, then sat down, hanging his head. "I don't feel up to staying out tonight," he said. "I think I'll just go sleep in my bed."

Hieronymus burst into tears. "Oh, you're so thin and weak," he sobbed. "Now you're hallucinating. I'm afraid if you don't eat something soon . . ."

Anton looked up. "Eat what?" he said. "The rope's not doing much for you, my friend. You're all skin and bones."

"It's true," the mouse wailed. "We're wasting away."

"Well, you'll make yourself worse, crying about it."

Hieronymus nodded, wiping his tears on his forepaws, then followed Anton's weaving trail down the gangway and into the captain's quarters. Anton settled himself on the pillow in the crate. "I'm so tired," he said. "I think I may just go to sleep forever."

Hieronymus sat down in front of him. "I've been thinking," he said. "Clearly you can't go on much longer, nor can I. So the time has come for nature to take its natural course between us. I won't resist. I ask you, as a friend—for truly you've become that to me, though I never would have believed such a thing could happen—I ask you to make it swift."

Anton contemplated the mouse dreamily. "Make what swift?" he asked.

"I'm offering myself to you. As a meal."

Anton chuckled. "You must be joking."

"I was never more serious," said Hieronymus, sitting up on his hind legs to achieve maximum height. "Why should we both die, if one might live?"

"Eating you isn't going to keep me alive," said Anton. "It would probably only make me throw up and waste more of my strength."

Hieronymus considered this. "Do you think so?"

"Nothing against you, but rodents always do make me sick. I can't bear the taste. And you're not exactly any cat's idea of a meal. There's no meat on you."

"So you won't accept my offer."

"You saved our lives, gnawing through that barrel. You said yourself, we're friends. Well, I don't eat my friends. Forget this idea of sacrifice. It's not in your nature. What would Great-Granduncle Portymus say?"

"You're right. I can't give up," the mouse said. "It's not in my nature. There must be a way to save us both."

"If there is," Anton agreed, "I trust you to find it." Then he yawned widely, showing all his teeth. "I can't stay awake," he said.

"I'm going back on deck," said the mouse. "I'll keep an eye out for fish."

On deck Hieronymus found that the weather

had changed, as so often happened at sea. The sky was cloudy, and the air had cooled noticeably. A light breeze played in the sails, not enough to fill them, but they rustled beneath the spars. As he looked up at the moon, which was shrouded in clouds, a thin beam of light broke through and seemed to shoot across the water to the ship. Then, as the mouse watched wide-eyed, the clouds parted, forming the pale lids of an enormous eye. It seemed to contemplate the ship, the deck, the mouse. Hieronymus felt the fur on his face tingle, and his spine shuddered. "The cat's eye," he murmured. What did it mean?

Where the eye sees the eye, he thought. That's what Anton was waiting for. It meant what was lost would be found. And weren't he and Anton lost? He rushed to the rail and looked out over the water, but it was dark, and though the moon shed upon it a pearly light, there was, as far as he could see, only water, water, and more water.

A profound sleepiness came upon Hieronymus as he turned back toward the cabin. He should tell Anton about this eye. He would want to know. Hieronymus made his way down the gangway and into the cabin, where Anton lay on the cushion

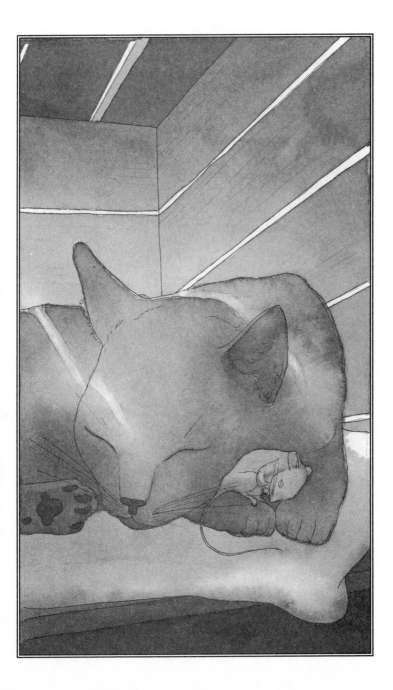

snoring sonorously. "Anton," he said softly. "The cat's eye."

But Anton was deep in sleep and it seemed a shame to disturb him. *I'll tell him when he wakes up,* Hieronymus thought. *I'm so tired all of a sudden. I may as well have a little nap.* And so the talkative, brave little mouse, the last descendant of a noble clan, curled up between the paws of the cat and fell asleep.

CHAPTER 14

Where the Eye
Sees the Eye

T he small dinghy crew grunted in surprise, looked back at the *Leone* in the distance, then squinted again at the ship before them. It sat motionless in the channel, its sails hanging untrimmed. Nobody at all was on deck—it appeared to the sailors to be completely abandoned.

"Er, what do we do now?" one of the men asked the first mate.

The first mate glanced at the two islands and back at the ship in front of them. He nodded straight ahead. "Let us have a look aboard,

215

shall we? Could be easy pickings, it could." The other men chuckled and resumed rowing. Strange islands gave them the creeps, but an abandoned ship—that was much more to their liking.

Cecil was infinitely relieved. As the space between the islands came into view he had watched the Eye carefully. It had not moved and now was fixed directly above the ship. He felt sure it had been over the ship all along. From beneath the bowsprit, a blue horse's head and forelegs surged forward, so it was not the ship Anton had left on, but Cecil still felt strangely drawn to it. The prickling feeling extended to his paws.

As they rowed strongly through the waves, Cecil was the first to notice something moving in the water near the ship, just below the surface, creating a shallow sort of current as it went. Whatever it was moved in a constant slow circle around the ship, the V in the water above it charting its path. Eventually a crewman saw it, too.

"What's that, eh?" he asked, craning his neck. "Not a shark I hope?"

Oh, cat's whiskers, thought Cecil with a pang in his belly. *I know what that is.*

"Dolphin, maybe?" said another.

On the next pass, the first mate saw what Cecil had already figured out.

"It's a whale," he said tersely. "Stop rowing. Be still."

The crew froze in mid-motion, no sound but the lapping of the waves on the sides of the dinghy. Cecil stood on his hind legs with one front paw on the edge, straining to see the whale, wondering if it could possibly be the same one he'd seen twice before. All the fur on his body felt like it was sticking straight out. The whale's huge head rolled into view, and it seemed to Cecil as if time slowed down. He saw the blue-gray skin and wide white jaw. He saw the deep blue eye with the crust of barnacles over it, looking out, finding him, filling him with that same sensation of wisdom and serenity that he remembered from that day on the schooner so long ago. *The eye,* thought Cecil with a kind of dreamlike clarity. Then the whale's eye looked straight up at the mysterious cloud-shrouded Eye in the sky. Cecil let out a little squeak. *This is it!* he thought. *This must be the other eye! The messenger. Of course.*

The whale turned and dipped below the surface again, the shallow current changing course and now moving directly toward the little boat. Suddenly the current vanished into a swirling eddy at one spot, and Cecil realized the whale must have dived straight down. One of the younger sailors stood up and screamed in terror, almost swamping them before the others were able to pull him down to his seat again. Cecil kept his balance and watched the water intently, trying to see under the waves.

The whale surfaced forcefully some distance behind them, and the panicked sailors paddled furiously toward the abandoned ship until they were even with it. Two pirates grabbed onto the ropes hanging limply over the side and shimmied up hand over hand, then secured more ropes and threw them over to the others. Cecil steeled himself to try another desperate rope climb, remembering all too well how the one on the side of the *Mary Anne* turned out, but the first mate swiftly slipped a hand under Cecil's belly, tucked him into his blue vest, and began to climb up. Shivering and grateful, Cecil looked straight up into the sky to see the Eye above them. *The lost shall be found,* he thought anxiously, and he wished with all his might that the old saying would turn out to have a little bit of truth to it.

❖ ❖ ❖

Although Cecil was hopeful about the chances of something good happening on board, the crewmen were decidedly more wary, even fearful. They were a superstitious lot in general, and an abandoned ship was an odd thing for a pirate. On one hand, there was nobody to have to fight and everything available for looting, which was good. On the other, there was the pesky question of *why* it was abandoned in the first place. Where could the crew have gone? Was there a battle with another vessel? A terrible storm? A plague? Or was it something even more sinister and mysterious—a creature from the deep with many eyes and long tentacles, attacking the ship and making off with every last passenger? They would never know, but these kinds of thoughts made the dinghy crew tread carefully about the ship, speaking in low voices and glancing behind themselves often.

Cecil, however, jogged briskly from deck to deck searching for evidence of any living being. As soon as he had wriggled out of the first mate's vest and dropped onto the wooden planking, he thought he caught a familiar scent. Very faint and washed out, but here somewhere. The main deck was curiously empty of the usual stacks of barrels and crates. A feeling of vague alarm grew in his brain with a fog of worry.

The pirates found a stash of shiny implements to eat and drink with and stuffed them into bags, as well as clothing and a few small swords. Cecil paced impatiently until they opened the hatch to the hold, but there was no smell of Anton down there, and Cecil began to wonder if he wanted to find his brother so badly that he had imagined the scent to begin with. In the galley, two crewmen were rummaging through the shelves when Cecil stepped in.

"Why, would you look a' that," said one, pointing to a tall water barrel with a wire clasp on the top. "Gnawed clear through, ain't it?" he said, fingering a rough hole in the face of the barrel. A pool of water had gathered on the floorboard.

Cecil stared at the hole in the barrel as well, with a sinking feeling in his bones. That looked like the work of some rodent to him. If Anton were here, he wouldn't have let mice run wild on his ship. Cecil turned and trotted up to the main deck again. He searched the map room, peered down into every coil of rope, even climbed the rigging all the way up to the crow's nest in case Anton had been stranded up there, but it was just as unoccupied as everyplace else. Cecil looked up and found the Eye again, floating mildly in the misty clouds. It seemed more distant now, though surely he was closer to it, and in his frustration he felt as if it mocked him with its presence. *Where is he?* he thought furiously at the Eye. *Tell me what to do now!* But the Eye merely glowed silently.

Making his way slowly back down the lattice of rigging, which was much more difficult than climbing up, Cecil crossed the deck and went back below. He could hear movement in the hallway of the officers' quarters. In the largest room, with piles of rolled-up maps on the table and a fine long coat hanging on a stand, Cecil found his rescuer and another sailor on their knees on the floor, trying to pry open a large sea chest.

"It's no use, sir," said the sailor, leaning back on his heels and breathing heavily. "We can't budge it."

The first mate rested one elbow on his knee

and noticed Cecil sitting quietly in the doorway. "And what of you, Lucky Black?" he asked Cecil. "Where's your luck now, eh? Supposed to be findin' somethin', you are."

Cecil gazed at the man. He had no idea what he was saying, but it was clear that he was interested in the chest. Cecil stretched his neck, looking over the problem, and saw that the lid was carved all over with fishes, just like the one he'd once opened. To the surprise of the men, Cecil leaped on top of the chest and began pressing and pressing the fish with his paws. The first mate laughed and said, "Well, it seems our Black has gone fishing," but Cecil ignored him. Was it this one? Or this one, maybe near the corner, then, BINGO, he felt a fish give beneath his paws. The latch released, and as Cecil leaped back to the floor, the lid snapped open.

The sailor gave a shout. "I'll be shivered," said the first mate. "Did you see that? Black, you've got more than luck on your side. I'm thinking you've got brains."

Cecil could see the men were excited, but he had no interest in the chest. It had no scent of

Anton. As they pulled the lid open and stood looking wide-eyed at the contents, Cecil hurried off down the hallway.

He passed a bedchamber and stopped to look in. This one contained a larger bed as well as a smaller one to fit a tiny human. There were several tall pieces of furniture, with drawers on the front and bottles and containers lined up on top. Cecil didn't want to try to jump up on one of them blindly, but he saw a box standing on end in a corner that would give him a better view. He sprang up on the box, turning to catch his balance as it wobbled unsteadily under his weight. As he faced the room again he saw a flash of movement at the far wall. He snapped his head and focused his eyes—it was a cat! His heart pounded crazily in his chest. One, two, three seconds passed before he recognized the feline, but it was not Anton. It was Cecil himself, his furry black reflection staring back at him in a "meer" like the one he had seen on the ship with Gretchen. The glass was attached to the wall across the room, and Cecil saw that he looked just as bad as he felt. He sat back slowly and began to breathe again, closing his eyes and dropping his head as disappointment poured over him in a great wave. It sure smelled like his brother in here, but he was nowhere in sight.

Maybe Anton was *here, but he left with the others,* Cecil thought. *Maybe I'll have to find out what happened to them.* He swallowed with difficulty. This could not be the end of his search—*it would not be.* He opened his eyes to try to clear his head and focus his thoughts, and was surprised to see a tiny flicker of light somewhere beneath him. It was strange, like a reflection in water, pale green and still. He shuffled his paws back and lowered his head, squinting down. There were narrow slats in the box, and it seemed like the glint of light was coming from inside, down near the bottom. Cecil lay one eye directly on the space between the slats and peered in, and the pale green light blinked.

It was a green eye, looking up at him.

In an instant Cecil had bounded to the floor and dashed around to the open back of the crate. He stood with his legs wide apart to steady himself, gulping in air and laughing. "Hey!" he managed to gasp out, his eyes bright with tears. "Where have you been, little kit?"

Anton lay in the crate, his chest rising and

falling, gazing intently at Cecil. "Wanted to see what it is they sing about," he whispered, smiling. He tried to get to his feet but slumped back into the cushion. Cecil realized with another shock how thin and frail Anton was. He stepped closer and touched Anton's nose quickly with his own, breathing in the familiar scent of his brother.

"Mother sent me to find you," Cecil said. "I promised her I would."

Hieronymus crept slowly out from between Anton's paws and tried to fix his eyes on the large cat looming above him. Cecil wiped his face with his paw and looked down at the mouse.

"What's this? A little snack," he said. He popped out his claws.

Anton held up a paw feebly. "That snack is a friend of mine. He saved my life."

"It's true," Hieronymus squeaked up at Cecil. "If not for me, he would have been a goner." Hastily, he retreated behind Anton.

Cecil looked back at Anton and nodded. How had a mouse saved his poor brother? It was a story he would want to hear. "Any friend of yours is a friend of mine," he said.

From down the hallway, they heard the shouts

of the pirates: "Huzzah!" and "It's gold, it's pure gold," and then the stamping of boots going from door to door, the first mate shouting, "Lucky Black, where are you, lad? You're the hero of the day."

"He's a kindly one," Cecil said to Anton. "He actually saved me from drowning. We've got to get him to take you off with us."

Anton sat up, staggered out of the box, and sat down again. Cecil licked his brother's cheeks and forehead. "You've been too sick to clean yourself," he said.

The first mate looked in the door, and seeing the two cats (but not the mouse hiding behind the pillow), called out to his fellow pirates, who came ambling joyfully behind him, "Here's our hero, and he's found a poor abandoned chum." Cecil mewed and rushed to his boots, then back to Anton—lick, lick, *can't you see he's my brother?*—then back to the boots, *meow, meow, meeeoooow!*

The first mate laughed. "I hear you, Black," he said. "We'll take your friend. The gold in that chest is heavy, but he don't appear to weigh much, so we'll squeeze him in." And with that the mate picked Anton up by his scruff, put him inside his vest, and strode out to the deck, where the pirates, having thrown down a rope ladder to the dinghy, were busily loading the sacks of gold doubloons they'd found in the chest. Cecil clambered down with a little help from the crewmen. No one saw the mouse who ran down a line at the stern and bolted under the seat, where he found, to his delight, an old sea biscuit, which he munched on joyfully all the way to the ship.

✤ ✤ ✤

From a corner of the cage, Gretchen watched the two brothers squabble over the plan. *Hero today, gone tomorrow,* she thought. The pirates' gratitude for the gold, like everything else about them, had proved fitful and unreliable. That first night they'd been so overjoyed, the cook had broken out three tins of the oily little fish and presented them in three separate pans. Hieronymus—*that mouse!*—insisted that Anton hide a few of his under the stove, as he was too weak to eat them all at once. For a few days, the cats could do no wrong, and every pirate hand was outstretched with a treat, every pirate's ugly face contorted in something resembling a smile when a cat came into view. Then the time came to divide up the gold, and no pirate was content with his share. Cats were no longer of interest, though they still got the dinner leftovers slapped down in one pan and all the dishwater they could drink. Another week passed and open hostility was running rife in the crew—in the wrong place at the wrong time a cat could get kicked. No sooner had they spotted land than the captain gave an order and the friends found themselves, all three plus *that mouse,* in a cage in a sprawling animal market on the edge of a bustling port city. *Again,* thought Gretchen ruefully.

Anton had made a good recovery, though he was never going to be a big, strong, muscle-headed guy like his brother. He was quicker and smarter, Gretchen thought. He was a tough cat, not like a fighter, but like a survivor. Seeing them together again made her heart feel light and happy. *The brothers,* she called them in her thoughts. The brothers were bickering now. Cecil paced up and down, as much as he could in the narrow space.

"You haven't been in a 'markit' like this before," he advised Anton pompously. "Gretchen and I have, and we know what to do."

"But . . ." began Anton.

"The thing to do is," Cecil continued, "whenever somebody comes by, lie down and act like you're sick or dying. That way we won't be traded away. We'll stay with the pirates. We need to stick together, not to be separated all over the world again." He stopped pacing and sat down to face them.

Anton tried again. "But, are we sure we really *want* to stick with the pirates? I mean, they don't seem overly fond of us—they're eager to trade us off at the first opportunity. Maybe we could find a better life than that." He noticed Hieronymus, who was able to slip in and out of the cage easily because of his size, trying to get his attention from the shadows.

"The pirates are fine!" Cecil exclaimed, pacing again. "Lots of food, lots of excitement."

"Lots of danger," Gretchen commented quietly, watching Anton. She felt oddly protective of him, something she wasn't used to feeling about anyone except herself.

Hieronymus sidled up next to Anton's forepaw, glancing nervously at Cecil before speaking. "I've examined the latch. It's made of wood, a wooden peg slipped through a hole in another peg," he explained to Anton. "I could try gnawing through it, if you think that might work." They exchanged a glance, almost a wink.

"Work?" Cecil snorted in Anton's direction. "No offense to your friend, but that'd take forever."

"It could," said Anton, amused.

"It would," said Hieronymus, "but it seems worth a try anyway." He turned and slipped through the ragged slats of the cage and made his way around to the latch, where he set to chewing.

The keeper of the market was a short man with long hair braided down his back and necklaces of painted wooden beads stacked on his chest. Brandishing a long stick made of cane, he strode back and forth calling out to potential customers, whacking the stick sharply on the tops of the cages of braying or mewling animals. Gretchen tried to strike up a conversation with a few of the other creatures, but none of them were friendly.

"I can't get any of these other prisoners to tell me a thing," she remarked to Cecil. After several hours of languishing in the sweltering stall, Gretchen was finding the routine of dutifully falling into a realistic dead faint whenever a human strolled by tiresome. Hieronymus had worked industriously on the wooden latch while avoiding the keeper, who periodically spotted him and hit the front of the cage with his stick, but the mouse had made little progress.

Leaning toward Cecil, Gretchen lowered her voice. "Are you sure we shouldn't be trying to find a new home, like Anton said?" she asked him.

"Not if it means getting split up again," Cecil replied, glancing anxiously at Anton, who was by the door encouraging the mouse's efforts. Gretchen could see the resolve on Cecil's face; he wasn't going to let Anton out of his sight if he could help it. "Nope, we're a team," he said. "Three heads are better than one!"

"Four!" squeaked Hieronymus from up front. Cecil rolled his eyes.

Anton was worried about the mouse's endurance. "You know, my friend," he said seriously, "you could just . . . go."

Hieronymus spat out a tiny sliver of wood. "What do you mean, go?" he asked.

"You're not captive in this cage like we are," said Anton. "You have a chance to escape, and you should take it. Really, you should get out of here."

Hieronymus held up one paw. "I've pledged

my troth; I will not leave a friend in danger." The mouse gave him such a severe look that Anton retreated a bit, trying to think of something else to say. In the next moment, in the din of the stall, Anton heard a human's voice. He knew he had heard it before, somewhere, but *where?* He raised his head to listen.

"Yes, yes, I need a cat, mayhap more than one," a man was saying to the keeper, looking around at the creatures. "I have rats in my larder like you would not believe, such awful brutes!" Anton couldn't see his face and he didn't understand the words, but the voice drew him. Cecil saw the man peering into the cages and murmured to the others to get down, but Anton remained standing at the cage door.

"Anton! Get away from there!" Cecil whispered loudly.

"Just a minute," said Anton, stretching his neck to get a better look. "I think I know this one somehow."

"Come on, it could be anybody. It's too risky."

The man finally turned toward their cage, and Anton saw the tall, thin build and the puffy white beard, like a cloud passing by. It was Cloudy! Anton's mind raced. Cloudy, from his first ship, for whom he had killed the fearsome rat, the cook who had treated him so kindly and given him the delicious little fishes. Surely he would remember the little gray cat. Anton leaped up with both paws pressed high on the cage door, meowing as loudly as he could. Cecil rose to tackle Anton if necessary.

"What are you doing?" demanded Cecil. "Don't call attention to yourself. You'll be traded for sure!"

"It's all right!" Anton assured him in between yowls. "He's a good one. He knows me." Anton was out of breath, but he kept yowling. "And," he gasped, turning to Cecil, "he knows *where I'm from.*"

Cecil and Gretchen stared at Anton for a long moment, absorbing the meaning of this statement, then hurtled themselves to the door, adding their voices to the clamor. Cloudy moved down the row to stand in front of the cage.

"Well, what's all this?" he asked, bending to look at their faces. "Quite a spirited group, aren't ye?" He caught sight of Anton and paused, furrowing his brow. "And who is this here? Have I met you before, little one?"

Anton thrust his paw through the slats, and

Cloudy gently grasped it. The cook touched the scar where the rat's teeth had sunk in and took in a sharp breath. He quickly looked to Anton's throat to confirm the deeper one there, then stepped back and smacked his hand on his forehead. "Bless my beard, it's Mr. Gray, is it? How the devil did ye end up here?" He blinked from Anton to the others. "Well, no matter, we've got to get ye out."

Cloudy collared the keeper and pointed to the cage. The three cats fell silent, suddenly fearful that only Anton would be chosen, but after haggling with the keeper, Cloudy seemed pleased enough to buy the whole lot. The cats huddled together, and Hieronymus stayed out of sight—tucked into the crook of Anton's elbow—as Cloudy paid a passing boy to cart the cage out of the market and into the fresh sea air of the docks.

❖ ❖ ❖

After the group had made their way back to the ship—there she was, the *Mary Anne*, her figure-head of the two little girls still dancing off the bow—the cats were given a quick meal in the galley. Hieronymus was able to slip safely into a dark corner, where he found plenty of crumbs to nibble. They quickly discovered why Cloudy was in need of aid. Cecil heard the noise first, his ears pivoting.

"Rats," he said with a mix of disdain and anticipation. "A fair number of them, I believe. In there." He nodded toward the larder.

"Ugh, rats," said Anton with a sigh. "I had a tough fight with one."

Cecil eyed Anton's scar approvingly. "You won, though, didn't you?"

Anton smiled. "Yes, brother," he said. "I was the victor."

Gretchen stepped up so all three stood side by side, facing the larder. They could hear faint clicking and twitching sounds coming from inside. "I ain't afraid of no stinkin' rats," she said fiercely. Cecil and Anton glanced at her with respect.

Cloudy followed the trio to the larder and opened the door. The cats barged in shoulder to shoulder, and Cecil raised his voice.

"All right, you nauseating lowlifes, your time on this ship is UP." The clicking sounds ceased completely; he had the rats' attention. "You know why we're here, and this will not be a pleasure cruise. We'll give you ONE CHANCE to save your worthless, revolting skins, but if you stupidly choose to stay, which would not be surprising given the puny size of your brains, then we're looking forward to what comes next." He paused, popped out his claws, and dragged them sharply across the wooden floorboard, leaving five distinct lines. Gretchen grinned and nodded slowly. Anton squared his shoulders and passed a paw over his cheeks, smoothing his whiskers.

"Count of three, then your time in this world is DONE," Cecil thundered, leaning forward. "One . . . two . . ." Simultaneously, the three cats crouched to spring.

There was an explosion in the larder as the rats bounded out of their hiding places, knocking boxes and tins off shelves, careening toward the doorway. Anton stepped aside and counted seven or eight of them as they streaked past. Cecil remained planted in the center of the small room so the rodents had to swerve around him, their claws scraping the floor as they scrambled. In seconds they were gone.

"My," said Gretchen, wide-eyed and smiling at the brothers. "That went well."

When the cats returned to the galley they found

Cloudy, who had briefly hopped up on the table as the rats rushed past, pouring milk from a tin into a large saucer for them. Anton spotted Hieronymus's eyes shining from the shadows in the corner, the mouse's little head nodding with pleasure.

"Wonderful!" Cloudy exclaimed, stroking each of them while they purred over the milk. "Better than I could have hoped for." He put his hands on his hips and leaned against the table, chuckling. "Mr. Gray, you have made some fine friends, you have. We shall enjoy our voyage now." He waved a large spoon over his head with a flourish. "Next stop, Lunenburg, Nova Scotia!"

And though our heroes could not understand him, dear reader, we know that this was very good news indeed.

❖ ❖ ❖

Two kittens hurried up the path to the lighthouse, tumbling and rolling as they went. It was tiring, but Billy had entrusted them with an important message, so they pushed on until they could see Sonya sitting on the brick apron by the back door. She was cleaning her tail with long strokes, and she looked up smiling when she heard them coming. Her kittens were only a few months old and so dear to her, with ears too big for their faces and skinny little tails. They were allowed to go exploring during the daylight hours, and she wondered what had these two in such a rush.

"Mama!" panted the black one, who arrived ahead of his sister. "Billy says to come!" A butterfly in the grass distracted him and he veered off.

"Why?" asked Sonya, as the second kitten, gray-striped, flopped down in a heap.

"Don't know why," she puffed. "He says to come *now*, Mama." She closed her eyes.

Sonya sighed. Billy had been very kind to her since Anton was taken and Cecil had followed. He helped her keep an eye on the kittens and checked on her often, and he let her know when a tall ship came in to the docks because there was always a chance of news of the brothers. But there had been no news, and it was hard not to lose hope. She left the kittens to rest at the lighthouse and started down the path at a trot. Hopeful was better than hopeless, she reminded herself, her heart aching a bit. She thought about her boys every day, whether a ship came in or not.

A crowd had gathered on the roadbed by the docks and Sonya wove her way toward the front, passing cats and people. She nodded to Mildred, the grandmother of Gretchen, that young white cat who had been taken. Mildred was unfailingly present no matter the weather when a big ship arrived, faithfully waiting for news of any kind, good or bad.

"Billy, what's going on?" asked Sonya when she found him near the water's edge. "Why all the fuss?"

Billy turned to her and beamed. "It's the *Mary Anne*. She's come back!" He was trying to contain his excitement and doing a very poor job of it.

"The *Mary Anne*?" Sonya repeated. "The ship that took Anton?" She felt suddenly light-headed and whipped around to find the ship in the distance. There it was, enormous and heaving in the waves under full sail, the little girls on the figurehead clearly discernible.

Mildred stepped up behind them and looked out as well. "Maybe we'll see your boy today?" she said softly.

Sonya moved a little nearer to the old cat for strength, her heart hammering in her chest. "We've gotten our hopes up before, haven't we? I'll believe it when I see it," she said quietly.

"She's coming about now," Billy called out

anxiously to the crowd, squinting intently at the ship.

Long seconds slipped by. The people milled about, chatting and pointing, but every cat on the wharf strained silently to see something, any sign of a familiar face on the *Mary Anne*. The great ship dipped majestically as it drew closer; some of the sailors were high up in the rigging pulling in the sails as others busily traversed the deck. And then, in the stillness that had gathered along the ground among the cats, Sonya heard a stirring sound. It was the long, joyful meow of a single cat, almost a howl, rising and falling. And then others to her right and left joined in, mewing cries of recognition and deep kindred spirit until it was a whole chorus of buoyant voices. Sonya felt her eyes begin to sting and cloud up.

"What is it, Bill?" she asked, her voice quavering. "I can't see a thing."

Billy opened his mouth and hesitated. "It's . . . *three*, my dear lady," he replied, almost in a whisper, nodding slowly, his eyes fixed on the ship. "Great cats above, it's all three."

Sonya's breath caught in her throat and she blinked hard to clear her eyes.

Finally she saw them, high up in the prow of the ship, sitting tall and proud, side by side, their heads lifted in the cool breeze, one gray, one white, and one black. What she couldn't see was a dapper little mouse, who stood boldly between the forepaws of the gray cat, talking nonstop.

As Sonya and Mildred and Billy leaned against one another to keep their knees from buckling, the great ship glided into the dockyard, unhurried, and the exultant song of the cats on the wharf rose to welcome their lost friends, found again and home at last.

ACKNOWLEDGMENTS

We want to thank our irrepressible and indefatigable agent, Molly Friedrich, and also our editor, Elise Howard, who entered into the spirit of the endeavor with the close attention and enthusiasm every writer hopes for.

We're also indebted to two very dear early readers, Roger Martin and John Cullen, for their patience, support, and humor throughout the long voyage to print.